What parts of the front cover picture are repeated in the design to the left?

How does the design show both stillness and movement?

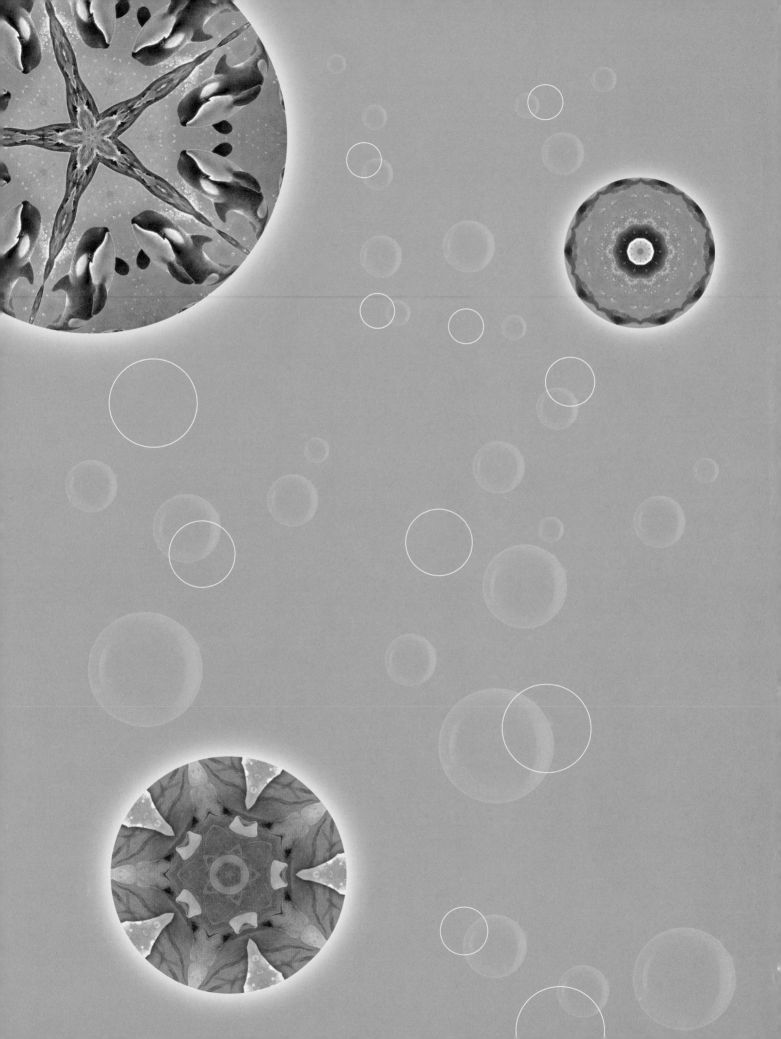

Literacy by Design™

Sourcebook
Volume 2

Program Authors
Linda Hoyt
Michael Opitz
Robert Marzano
Sharon Hill
Yvonne Freeman
David Freeman

Rigby®
A Harcourt Achieve Imprint

www.Rigby.com
1-800-531-5015

Welcome to Literacy by Design,
Where Reading Is...

Discovering

Questioning

Imagining

Literacy by Design: Sourcebook Volume 2
Grade 5

ISBN-13:   978-1-4189-4041-6
ISBN-10:   1-4189-4041-0

Printed in China
1 2 3 4 5 6 7 8   985 13 12 11 10 09 08 07 06

Thinking

Exploring

An *Expanding* Nation

THEME 10 Settling the West Pages 288–317

Modeled Reading

Shared Reading

Interactive Reading

v

UNIT ▷ Living With NATURAL FORCES

THEME **13** **Communication Revolution** Pages 382–411

Modeled Reading

Shared Reading

Interactive Reading

UNIT  Pulse of *Life*

THEME ⑮ Nature's Building Blocks
Pages 444–473

***Emigrants Crossing
the Plains, 1867***
Albert Bierstadt (1830–1902)

UNIT: An *Expanding* Nation

Viewing

The artist who painted this picture was Albert Bierstadt. He traveled the Oregon Trail where he photographed and sketched the scenery. He was famous for his large paintings of the American West.

1. Based on the landscape in the painting, what role do you think explorers played in helping settlers move west? Why do you think this?

2. What information does the painting supply about how settlers moved west?

3. Study the painting. What challenges do you think settlers faced on their journey?

In This UNIT

In this unit, you will read about how the United States expanded westward. You will learn the role explorers played in settling the West. You will also learn why and how settlers moved west.

Exploring the West

Contents

Modeled Reading

Shared Reading

Interactive Reading

BEWILDERED FOR THREE DAYS

As to Why Daniel Boone Never Wore His Coonskin Cap

written and illustrated by Andrew Glass

Precise Listening

Precise listening means listening for special word meanings. Listen to the focus questions your teacher will read to you.

Blazing
The Wilderness Trail

Daniel Boone

Dear Gram,

Dad says we're related to Daniel Boone. Is that true? I just learned about Daniel Boone in school. We're studying the **colonization** of territories west of the Appalachian Mountains. Way back in the 1770s, Boone cut a trail through the Cumberland Gap. I learned that settlers used the trail to move west to Kentucky. My teacher says that legends claim Daniel Boone didn't like to have neighbors too near. She said maybe that's why Boone blazed the trail. He wanted other people to be able to **escape** the **commotion** of city life. Hmmm. Maybe Dad IS related to him since Dad wants to escape city traffic!

Mom said it would be fun to take a car trip along the trail, since it starts not far from our town. It would be more fun if Dad would quit saying "**commence**." He read a quote by Boone in the book I'm reading— Boone says his friends always "commence" to whoop and holler—now Dad is walking around talking like Boone. (Can you see my eyes roll?) When we get to Kentucky, we're going to hike in the Cumberland Gap National Historical Park. Unlike Daniel Boone, we're taking a **compass**!

Love,

Robin

Structured Vocabulary Discussion

Work with a partner or in a small group to fill in the following blanks. Be sure you can explain how the words are related.

Coat is to *cold* as _____ is to *lost*.

Settlement is to _____ as *disturbance* is to _____.

Throughout the week, add to your vocabulary journal entries. Record new insights and other words that relate to this week's vocabulary.

Picture It

Copy this word wheel into your vocabulary journal. In the upper sections, name things you would want to **escape**. In the bottom sections, name things you would not want to escape.

Copy this word chart into your vocabulary journal. Fill in the lower left box with synonyms of **commence**. Fill in the lower right box with antonyms of commence.

commence	
synonyms	**antonyms**
start	end
_____	_____
_____	_____
_____	_____

(word wheel: center "escape"; sections labeled "danger", "fun")

Make Connections
Compare/Contrast Information

Sometimes you can make connections between something you read and something you have read, seen, heard, or done before by comparing and contrasting information. Identifying similarities and differences between your own experiences and what you are reading will help you understand information better.

When you COMPARE and CONTRAST INFORMATION, you show how things are similar and different.

Think about how text elements are similar and different as you read.

TURN AND TALK Listen as your teacher reads the following lines from *Bewildered for Three Days*. Then with a partner, read the lines and look for ways that you may make connections by comparing and contrasting information. Discuss answers to these questions.

- Have you ever read, seen, heard, or done anything that would compare to Daniel Boone's experience in the forest?

- What experiences have you had that would contrast with Daniel Boone's as described here?

What with all the zigging and zagging, and doubling back, I'd lost my bearings, and bedded down two more nights in the forest before finding my way home to Mama.

The painter dashed the last bits of color onto his canvas. He turned it around to show me the picture of myself holding a wide-brimmed hat.

"You mean to tell me that the great Daniel Boone was lost in the woods?" he asked.

"No sir," I replied. "I can't say that I was ever truly lost, only that I was bewildered for three days."

TAKE IT WITH YOU Comparing and contrasting information will help you enjoy and understand what you read. As you read other selections, look for ways that you can compare or contrast what you are reading with something you have read, seen, heard, or done before. Use a chart like the one below to help you compare and contrast information.

Item 1 Daniel Boone

Item 2 My Camping Trip

Differences

- spent the night in the woods for two nights by himself
- would not admit he was lost
- told the story to a painter who was painting his picture
- made a joke about his experiences

Similarities

- both of us got lost from our families
- both had our pictures made
- both made a joke about what happened

Differences

- I got lost at Yellowstone while I was camping with my family.
- I was lost for a couple of hours and I was scared.
- Some people took me to the Ranger Station.
- I laughed about being lost, after it was over, and got my picture in my school newspaper for having an exciting summer adventure.

From Sea to Shining Sea

by M. J. Cosson

Oregon Trail

In the early 1800s, the land between the Mississippi River and the Pacific coast was untamed. Native Americans had lived there for thousands of years, but they did not believe in owning land. The U.S. government did. And so did the American people. The country wanted to grow, and that growth required land. The United States looked west for land.

In 1803, the United States paid France $15 million for the Louisiana Purchase. The land purchased stretched from the Mississippi River to the Rocky Mountains. The United States got Florida in a deal with Spain in 1821. War with Mexico gave the United States lands in the Southwest and California. By 1850, the United States stretched from sea to sea.

As the country grew west, people followed. Fur trappers were among the first Americans to head west. The trappers hunted and trapped and set up trade with Native Americans. In the process, they helped explore the uncharted West.

California

Santa Fe Trail

SANTA FE TRAIL

Rocky Mountains

Settlers also wanted to move west. And they needed a way to get there. Thus, trails played a major role in settling the West. The Santa Fe Trail was one of the first trails. It began in 1821 as a trade route. The trail ran between Independence, Missouri, and Santa Fe, New Mexico. Millions of dollars worth of goods traveled over the trail. The Oregon Trail also began in Independence. It crossed the Rocky Mountains. Between 1841 and 1869, about half a million people took the trail. Most went to Oregon or California.

Throughout the 1800s, millions of people headed west across the continent. Some hoped to get rich through trade, commerce, or gold. Some went for the unlimited adventure or to escape debts or other troubles. Some went to spread their religion or to find a place where they could worship freely. Most hoped for a better life. They all bravely faced hunger, weather, sickness, death, and untold dangers to make new lives on new land.

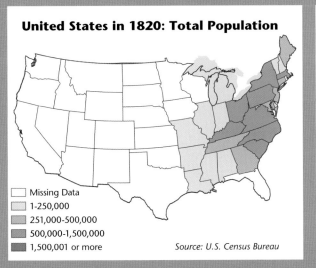

United States in 1820: Total Population

Missing Data
1-250,000
251,000-500,000
500,000-1,500,000
1,500,001 or more

Source: U.S. Census Bureau

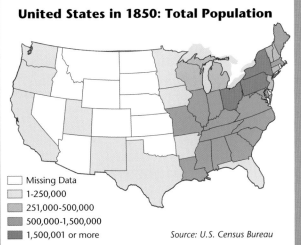

United States in 1850: Total Population

Missing Data
1-250,000
251,000-500,000
500,000-1,500,000
1,500,001 or more

Source: U.S. Census Bureau

Pikes Peak

A mountain that is unexplored?
We'll reach its peak today!
Unstoppable is how I feel,
So I will lead the way.

My men can't climb; they're unprepared,
But somehow I don't mind.
I'm unconcerned with coats and food,
We leave them all behind.

Night temperatures begin to fall,
The peak is still not near.
Uneven rocks are unfit beds,
Unmentioned is our fear.

The morning is unpromising,
Unequipped for all this snow.
Unannounced and unfulfilled,
Back down to camp we go.

In 1806, Zebulon Pike spotted a blue peak rising high in the Rocky Mountains. Pike and several men tried to reach the top. Cold and snow forced them back. Climbers finally scaled Pikes Peak in 1820.

Prefix *un-*

Activity One

About the Prefix

A prefix is a word part added to the beginning of a root word to make a new word. The prefix *un-* usually means "not." *Unsuccessful* means "not successful." As your teacher reads *Pikes Peak*, listen for the prefix *un-* at the beginning of words.

Prefix in Context

With a partner, read *Pikes Peak* to find words with the prefix *un-*. Write the word in a chart like the one below. Then, use your understanding of prefixes to write the definition of each word.

WORDS WITH PREFIX *UN-*	DEFINITION
unexplored	not explored

Activity Two

Explore Words Together

Look at the list of the words on the right. Add the prefix *un-* to each word to make a new word. Tell a partner the meaning of one of the words on your list and have him or her name the word. For example, you might say "This word means 'not reasonable,'" and your partner would answer, "Unreasonable." Then switch roles.

reasonable	educated
aware	noticed
concerned	knowing

Activity Three

Explore Words in Writing

Write a paragraph about a time when you felt unstoppable. Use at least three words with the prefix *un-* in your paragraph. Share your writing with a partner.

Thank You, Lewis and Clark!

by Tisha Hamilton

"This is so much fun," 10-year-old Diane Shaw called to her twin brother Andre. Andre looked up and grinned. They were paddling smoothly, sending their canoes slicing through the steady current of the Missouri River. At the moment Andre and Diane were traveling side by side in separate canoes. Diane sat in one canoe along with her mother and half of the Shaws' camping supplies. Andre and his father were in an identical canoe with the other half of their gear.

Traveling upstream was slower than going downstream. But that was how the Shaws liked it. They thought it was worth the extra effort and time in order to really see everything the river had to offer. This section of the Missouri was part of the National Wild and Scenic River trail. That meant it was part of the original route followed by the explorers Lewis and Clark. It was also the longest stretch of unspoiled land along the Missouri. There was a lot to see.

Have you ever been on a camping or canoe trip? What is similar or different about your experience and that of the twins here?

The family had started out yesterday in Kipp State Park, Montana. Canoeing along this part of the Missouri River was like traveling in a wide canyon. The steep walls of the valley rose on either side. The walls had black shale on the bottom and yellow sandstone at the top.

The scenery was more than unmoving cliffs and stone, though. There was an unbelievable amount of wildlife, too. The Shaws were startled the first time a beaver slapped its broad tail in the water as the canoes went by. Now they were used to it. Diane had already spotted a bald eagle soaring overhead. Andre had been thrilled to see his first pelican. It had stretched its enormous wings as it flew low along the water, searching for its next meal. Everywhere the family saw ducks, geese, and deer.

Compare and contrast the wildlife you have read about or seen with the wildlife described on this page.

Later, the family might see bighorn sheep and elk. There were even dinosaur beds farther upriver. In the meantime, the Shaws were concentrating on Lewis and Clark. They were stopping at campsites along the way.

Mrs. Shaw liked to read from the journals of Lewis and Clark. She told the family that in 1803, President Jefferson had asked Meriwether Lewis to map the Missouri River. Lewis had formed a group known as the Corps of Discovery. William Clark helped lead the group. The group included skilled boatmen. Along the way they were joined by a French interpreter and his Native American wife, Sacagawea. Sacagawea's baby made the trip. So did Lewis's dog. The group did not have an atlas to guide the way. They were traveling in uncharted lands. What an adventure!

The group relied on food found along the way, mostly beaver and deer. One of Sacagawea's contributions was her knowledge of native plants. She knew how to identify them, where to find them, and how to prepare them. These plants added much-needed variety to the group's diet.

After hearing about the plant gathering, Diane had been excited to find a wild licorice plant at one of the stops. It was one of the plants Sacagawea collected. Diane took a picture of the plant. "Thank you!" she exclaimed.

Say Something Technique Take turns reading a section of text, covering it up, and then saying something about it to your partner. You may say any thought or idea that the text brings to your mind.

How are the experiences of the Shaw family similar to or different from the experiences of the Corps of Discovery?

On their third day, the Shaws came to a fork in the river. Using his compass, Andre determined that one fork flowed more from the north and one fork flowed more from the west. Both forks definitely looked like they could be the Missouri River.

Giving his parents a perplexed look, Andre asked, "What should we do now?"

"These rivers are like you and Diane," his mother pointed out. "They're almost twins." It was true—it seemed impossible to tell which side was the Missouri, and which was just another river that joined it.

"I don't think the Lewis and Clark journals can help us here," Diane sighed, shaking her head.

"Actually, they can," Mrs. Shaw informed her children. "This must be the place the Corps named Decision Point, where they also had to decide which river to follow."

The family pulled over to the riverbank and pored through the books about the Corps they'd brought with them. They learned that the Corps had camped between the two rivers for 10 days while they tried to figure out which way to go. Ten long, unforgettable days!

Have you ever had to choose between two paths? How is your experience similar to or different from the Shaws' decision?

The journals showed that the Corps had explored many miles up each fork to figure out which way to go. Native Americans had described an unusual waterfall on the Missouri. If the group could find the waterfall, they'd know they were on the right fork.

"Lewis finally located the Great Falls of the Missouri on the west river," Andre read. "He named the other river for his cousin Maria. Neat!"

"After that it was called Maria's River," his father agreed. "Then later on they took out the apostrophe. Today it's called the Marias River."

Have you ever used history or historical facts to help you know something in real life? Explain your answer.

"I'm just glad we don't have to hike for miles and miles to figure out which way to go," Diane said.

"Lewis and Clark did that so we wouldn't have to," her mother reminded her.

"Thank you, Meriwether Lewis and William Clark!" Andre and Diane chorused as they climbed back in their canoes.

Think and Respond

Reflect and Write

- You and your partner have read sections of *Thank You, Lewis and Clark!* and said something about it to each other. Discuss the thoughts and ideas you shared.

- Choose two connections you made to the story. Write them on one side of an index card. On the back of the card, write the similarities and differences between the story and your experiences.

Prefixes in Context

Reread *Thank You, Lewis and Clark!* to find examples of words with the prefix *un-*. Then work with a partner to use the words to create a postcard message describing the twins' Missouri River adventure. Share your postcard with the class.

Turn and Talk

MAKING CONNECTIONS: COMPARE/CONTRAST INFORMATION

Discuss with a partner what you have learned about how to compare and contrast information when you make connections.

- What does it mean to compare and contrast information?

- How can making connections by comparing and contrasting help you understand your reading better?

Review with a partner *Thank You, Lewis and Clark!* Choose a connection you made between the Shaw family and something you had read, seen, heard, or done before. Discuss how comparing and contrasting helped you understand the story.

Critical Thinking

With a partner, brainstorm a list of skills you would need in order to survive in the wilderness. Look back at *Thank You, Lewis and Clark!* Then write answers to these questions.

- How is travel in a wilderness area of the western United States easier today than it was 200 years ago?

- In what ways did the Corps of Discovery and other explorers benefit later settlers and the United States overall?

Arch on Missouri River

SACAGAWEA

WILDERNESS GUIDE Sacagawea (sa-CA-ga-we-uh) was the only female member of the Lewis and Clark expedition. The young Shoshone and her husband joined the group in 1804. Sacagawea made many **contributions** to the group's success. She helped the group gain the support of Native Americans they met. She also helped the group find its way. This was important, since Lewis and Clark did not have an **atlas** to guide them to the Pacific Coast.

BABY ON BOARD Sacagawea and her husband had a baby son nicknamed Pomp. Pomp was Sacagawea's constant traveling **companion**. She kept Pomp strapped to her back in case the group had to **flee** danger.

CALM IN A CRISIS The group often traveled in a **caravan** of canoes and flat-bottom boats. One day, Sacagawea's husband tipped one of the boats. Papers and other important items flew into the water. Sacagawea reacted quickly. She was able to save most of the items.

Structured Vocabulary Discussion

When your teacher says a vocabulary word, have the people in your group take turns saying the first word they think of. Continue until your teacher says, "Stop." Then have the last person who said a word explain how his or her word is related to the vocabulary word.

Throughout the week, add to your vocabulary journal entries. Record new insights and other words that relate to this week's vocabulary.

Picture It

Copy this word organizer into your vocabulary journal. Fill in the boxes with ways people might make **contributions** to society.

contributions
People can volunteer their time at a homeless shelter.

Copy this word web into your vocabulary journal. Fill in the circles with groups that might travel in a **caravan**.

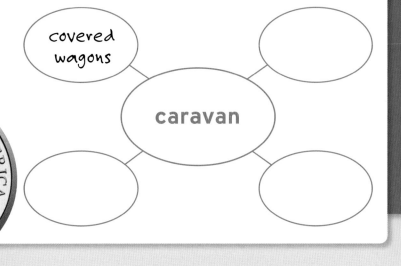

covered wagons

caravan

Cumberland Gap

traditional song

Cumberland Gap is a traditional song from the Cumberland area of the Appalachian Mountains. It is written in a regional dialect that reflects the speech of the time. The Cumberland Gap was the first great gateway to the West. As such, it symbolizes the pioneer spirit of men like Daniel Boone who braved the unknown to open new lands to settlers.

Me and my wife and my wife's pap,
We're all going down to Cumberland Gap.
Me and my wife and my wife's pap,
We're all going down to Cumberland Gap.

Chorus:
Cumberland Gap, Cumberland Gap.
Hey! Flee down yonder to Cumberland Gap.

Cumberland Gap with its cliffs and rocks
Home of the panther, bear, and fox.
Cumberland Gap with its cliffs and rocks
Home of the panther, bear, and fox.

Cumberland Gap is a mighty fine place,
Three kinds of water to wash your face.
Cumberland Gap is a mighty fine place,
Three kinds of water to wash your face.

Boone cut a trail through Cumberland Gap,
A felt hat on his head, not a coonskin cap.
Boone cut a trail through Cumberland Gap,
A felt hat on his head, not a coonskin cap.

Jim Beckwourth,
Mountain Man

Do you love the Old West almost as much as you love stamp collecting? If you do, we have the perfect stamp for you—Jim Beckwourth. Beckwourth wore many hats. He was a trapper, trader, guide, and first-rate storyteller. The stamp is part of the U.S. Postal Service's Black Heritage series. It will make an inexpensive but distinguished addition to anyone's stamp collection.

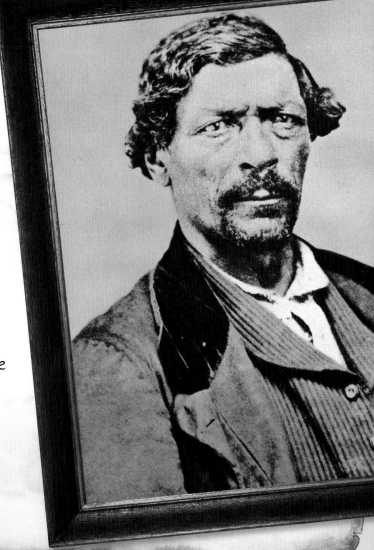

Jim Beckwourth was an independent man. Born a slave in Virginia in 1798, he moved to Missouri and eventually gained his freedom. But Beckwourth was unhappy in St. Louis. He disliked his job. So he joined a group of fur traders headed for the Rocky Mountains. This was the first of many adventures.

Beckwourth spent many years hunting and trapping. During part of his time he lived with the Blackfeet and Crow. The Crow even made him a chief. Many of Beckwourth's stories are tales of his time among Native Americans. Some of his claims are probably nonsense, but some may be true. We know that Beckwourth discovered a mountain pass that helped travelers reach California.

Prefixes *non-*, *in-*, and *dis-*

Activity One

About the Prefixes

Prefixes are word parts that can be added to the beginning of some root words. The prefixes *non-*, *in-*, and *dis-* usually mean "not." *Nonproductive* means "not productive," *informal* means "not formal," and *disinterested* means "not interested." As your teacher reads the article about Jim Beckwourth, listen for words with the prefixes *non-*, *in-* and *dis-*.

Prefixes in Context

With a partner, read *Jim Beckwourth, Mountain Man*. Find words with the prefixes *non-*, *in-*, and *dis-*. Write the prefixes and words in a chart like the one below. Then use what you know about prefixes to write the definition of each word.

PREFIX	WORD	DEFINITION
in-	independent	not dependent

Activity Two

Explore Words Together

With a partner, look at the list of words on the right. On separate cards, write the words. Write a definition for each word on another card. Mix up the cards. Take turns matching the correct definition with a word.

nonfiction	nonsense
independent	inexpensive
disagree	discomfort

Activity Three

Explore Words in Writing

Write a letter to convince the United States Postal Service to create a new stamp that honors your favorite explorer. Use at least three words with the prefixes *non-*, *in-*, or *dis-* in your letter. Exchange letters with a partner and circle the words with the prefixes.

The LIFE and TRAVELS of JEDEDIAH SMITH

retold by Elise Oliver

My name is Jedediah Strong Smith. I'm a simple man, so I'll try to make the telling of my life story simple, too. There are folks who'll tell you wild tales about me and the trouble I've been in, but I'm nothing special. I'm just an honest man who always tries to live right and do right by others.

I was born in the year 1799, on the 6th of January, in Bainbridge, New York. I grew up in Ohio and Pennsylvania. I didn't stick around there too long, though. I began to dream of seeing the world when I was still a youngster. I started traveling westward and the farther I got, the more I liked what I saw. I loved the huge mountains that seemed to touch the sky, their peaks disappearing into the clouds. Now, if you've never seen the Rocky Mountains, that's something you've got to do. There's nothing quite like a sunrise over the Rockies. The sun bursts over the mountains in gold and orange and red, and it looks like the whole world is on fire.

What strategies could you use to understand what Jedediah Smith means by the words "simple" and "special"?

What is a "travel route"? Explain what strategies would help you find out the meaning.

In 1822, I signed up with a trapping outfit out of Missouri—trapping, that's the fur business, you know. I spent my time trapping beaver, fox, mink, and the like and selling their hides for a good price. It's hard, dangerous work. You're out in snow waist deep, the wind howling, your feet frozen like two blocks of ice. You never know what's going to be there waiting for you around every corner. Could be a good fur catch, could be something waiting to catch you. A bear could jump out of the woods and try to eat you for dinner. I've lost many men to attacks over the years. I found myself in the very jaws of a bear once. It would have killed me if I hadn't decided to play dead. It took one of my men hours to stitch me up with a needle and thread.

Anyway, I figured the trapping and trading business was a good way for me to earn a living. It was a good way to see the West, too. I spent some time in the Rocky Mountains. And I got a taste for discovering travel routes and passages through the wild.

Reverse Think-Aloud Technique Listen as your partner reads part of the text aloud. Choose a point in the text to stop your partner and ask what he or she is thinking about the text at that moment. Then switch roles with your partner.

In 1826, I left the shore of the Great Salt Lake in Utah and joined 15 other trappers in a caravan headed south. We reached the mighty Colorado River in October. We kept going until we got to the Mojave Desert. We were starving and parched from thirst. The hot wind blew nonstop. Our horses died and we had to walk for miles. The kindness of the folks at the mission of San Gabriel saved us from an insufferable fate.

Beaver trapping was good along the California coast. My men and I could have stayed on there and been happy. But the Mexican government wouldn't let us trade there. So we packed up and traveled north through the Central Valley of California.

What fix-up strategy could you use if you did not know the meaning of the word "parched"?

We made it to the Sierra Nevada by May. It was cold up in those mountains at night! Then we struggled through the harsh Nevada desert on our way back to Utah. In July 1827, we returned to the Great Salt Lake, the exact spot where we had started the year before.

My best friend in those days was Harrison Rogers. He had been my companion on the California run. Without resting long in Utah, Rogers and I hired a team of trappers and went back out on the trail. We started out following our same route south toward the Mojave Desert.

How can you understand what Smith means by "run" in this passage?

Sadly, disaster was soon upon us. We were attacked on the trail before we even reached California. Half the men in our party died. The rest of us went on, but many of us were discouraged.

Our trapping party then traveled up through central California to the Pacific Coast. There we saw redwood trees as big around as small houses. As we continued north through Oregon, we again ran into trouble. Most of our group died, including my good friend Harrison Rogers. Only three of us survived. In August 1828 we finally arrived in Canada. Our difficult journey had come to an end.

In 1829, I had some family business in the East. So I decided to sell my share of the Rocky Mountain Fur Company. I started thinking about settling down. The next year I bought myself a house in St. Louis. Now I have one more run down the Santa Fe Trail, and my traveling days will be over.

Well, that's my life, up until now. Thanks for listening to my story. Remember, there's always a new trail to blaze.

What fix-up strategy could you use to understand what Smith means by "blaze"?

In May 1831 Jedediah Strong Smith died while searching for water along the Santa Fe Trail. He was 32 years old.

Think and Respond

Reflect and Write

- You and your partner took turns reading parts of *The Life and Travels of Jedediah Smith* and sharing what you were thinking. Discuss your thoughts and their relationship to the story.

- On index cards, write three unfamiliar words from the text. On the backs of each index card write what fix-up strategy you used to figure out that word's meaning. Compare your cards with your partner's.

Prefixes in Context

Reread *The Life and Travels of Jedediah Smith* to find examples of the prefixes *non-*, *in-*, and *dis-*. Write down the words you find. Then include the words in a brief description of Jedediah Smith. Exchange descriptions with a partner. Then, circle the prefixes in your partner's description.

Turn and Talk

USE FIX-UP STRATEGIES

Discuss with a partner what you have learned so far about fix-up strategies.

- What are some examples of fix-up strategies?

- How do you use fix-up strategies to increase understanding?

Choose one problem you had while reading *The Life and Travels of Jedediah Smith*. Explain to a partner what fix-up strategy you used to solve the problem.

Critical Thinking

With a partner, discuss how Jedediah Smith's life was hard and dangerous. Write a list of dangers and hardships he faced during his life. Then write answers to these questions.

- Do you think Smith enjoyed the life of a trapper?

- Do you think Smith thought the good parts of being a trapper outweighed the bad parts? What elements of the story lead you to this conclusion?

- What modern-day jobs might create similar feelings for people who do them?

Contents

Modeled Reading

Shared Reading

Interactive Reading

THE WAY WEST

JOURNAL OF A PIONEER WOMAN

by Amelia Stewart Knight

Strategic Listening

Strategic listening means listening to make sure you understand the selection. Listen to the focus questions your teacher will read to you.

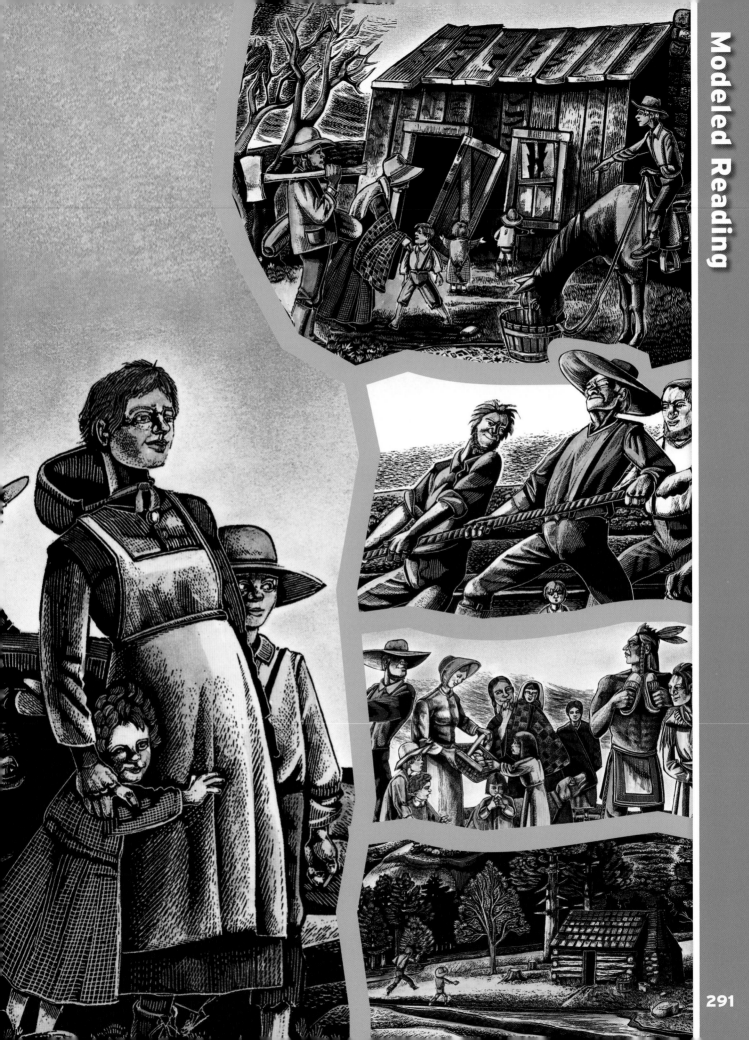

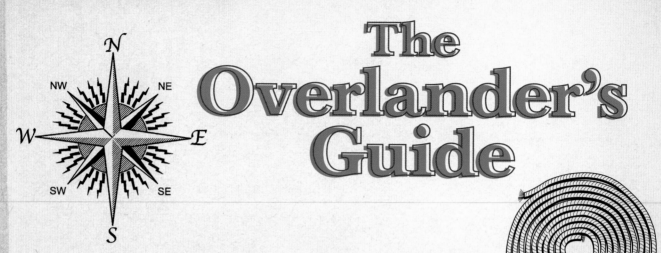

The Overlander's Guide

Are you itching to join the **expansion** westward? Do you dream of being a **pioneer** in Oregon? Do not be fooled by idle talk. Careful preparation for the journey is your key to success.

FOOD SUPPLIES: People will tell you that you can hunt for your food along the trail. Do not believe them. There are many **desolate** areas where buffalo do not live. Take twice as many supplies as you would need at home. At the least, each person should bring 200 pounds of flour, 100 to 150 pounds of bacon, 20 pounds of sugar, and 10 pounds of salt.

ARTICLES AND LIVESTOCK: Leave your furniture back east. Wagons loaded with heavy objects will not be able to **ascend** the mountains. Carry only your necessary pots, pans, eating utensils, and bedding. Bring tents and poles, shovels, axes, spades, and hoes. Make sure you have plenty of rope. Check your wagon; it needs to be sturdy. Also, consider the age of the horses you bring on the trail. Very young or very old horses do not do well on the **migration** west.

Structured Vocabulary Discussion

Work with a partner to complete the following sentences about your vocabulary words. When you are finished, share your answers with the class. Be sure you can explain how the words are related.

People believed in westward *expansion* because . . .

The *migration* of the buffalo meant that the animals . . .

To reach their home, the settlers had to *ascend* . . .

Throughout the week, add to your vocabulary journal entries. Record new insights and other words that relate to this week's vocabulary.

Picture It

Copy this word wheel into your vocabulary journal. Fill in the sections with words that describe a **pioneer**.

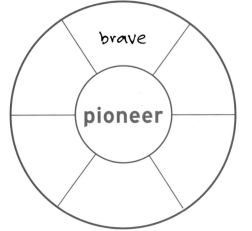

Copy this word organizer into your vocabulary journal. Fill in the ovals with words that mean the same as **desolate** and list examples of places that are desolate in the boxes.

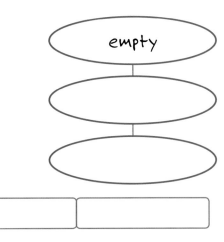

Infer

Author's Purpose

Look for clues in the words and pictures to help you figure out, or infer, the author's reason or reasons for writing. Inferring the author's purpose will help you understand what you read.

An **AUTHOR'S PURPOSE** is the reason for writing.

As you read, look for clues to help identify why an author wrote a passage or a piece.

TURN AND TALK Listen as your teacher reads the following lines from *The Way West*. Discuss with a partner the following questions.

• What clues tell you about the author's journey?

• Why do you think the author wrote the diary entries?

SATURDAY, SEPTEMBER 10, 1853. It would be useless for me to describe the awful road we have just passed over. . . . It is very rocky all the way, quite steep, winding, sideling, deep down, slippery and muddy. . . . and this road is cut down so deep that at times the cattle and wagons are almost out of sight. . . . the poor cattle straining to hold back the heavy wagons on the slippery road.

TUESDAY, SEPTEMBER 13, 1853. We are in Oregon, with no home, except our wagons and tent.

SATURDAY, SEPTEMBER 17, 1853. A few days later, my eighth child was born. We picked up and ferried across the Columbia River, utilizing skiff, canoes, and flatboat to get across, taking three days to complete.

TAKE IT WITH YOU Considering the author's purpose for writing will help you understand and enjoy what you read. As you read other selections, look for clues that help you infer why the author wrote a passage or piece. Use a chart like the one below to organize the clues.

In the Text	Author's Purpose	Why Do You Think That?
"It would be useless for me to describe the awful road we have just passed over."	To tell how hard it was to get to Oregon	Because she includes many details about the road
"A few days later, my eighth child was born."	To say that things worked out OK.	Because the last part of the trip was so hard and this was the happy ending
The Entire Text	To tell the story of her trip to Oregon so she could remember it later and share it with others.	Because the whole journal is devoted to telling what happened on the trip to Oregon

LAND RUSH!

by John Manos

Justin woke up before dawn with a start. He heard a wooden spoon rattling in an iron skillet. "Why are we getting up so early, Lucy?" he asked his sister. "It's hardly light!" Justin began to rearrange his bedroll.

"There is no such thing as 'too early' on the most important morning of our lives," Ma said as she walked by leading their horse, Babe. She winked at Justin, but her face was serious.

"It's going to be a beautiful day," Lucy said.

Justin thought about the thousands of people eagerly waiting with them at the borders of Oklahoma Territory. At noon today, April 22, 1889, everyone would make a frantic dash into the territory to claim free land. Justin wondered how many other families needed a new home in Oklahoma as desperately as his family did.

"Where do you reckon we'll end up?" Justin asked Ma.

"I'm headed for Guthrie," Ma said. "Meet me there. A widow can make a decent living in a town. And I have you and Lucy to help me."

Ma had carefully reviewed information about Guthrie before settling on it as her intended destination. She knew the railroad had a stop there and that people had previewed the town and divided it into lots.

"Do you think one of those lots will be ours?" Lucy asked, looking concerned.

"It all depends on how fast I can ride Babe," Ma answered. If Babe was faster than the other horses, then Ma could beat out the competition for a good site in town.

Justin spent the morning preparing Babe for the wild race across the Oklahoma plains. A half-hour before noon, he saddled the horse.

Lucy helped Ma into the saddle when 15 minutes remained. Ma moved Babe into position as Justin and Lucy stood on their wagon and stared at Pa's watch—each minute took a year!

Justin and Lucy heard the report of the cannon and a huge shout all along the line. Ma kicked Babe's sides sharply and burst away. Through a huge cloud of dust, Justin and Lucy could see Ma and Babe sprinting ahead of everyone else. They cheered until their throats were raw.

A New Town in Oklahoma

Aunt Clara Brown

Dear Aunt Clara,

Denver, Colorado, is even more wonderful than I imagined it would be. My family members have settled into our new home. Thanks to you, we now have a chance to rebuild our lives. I don't know how we can ever repay you for your kindness.

I recorded many of your stories about growing up in slavery in my diary as we traveled west from Kansas. My parents' lives in slavery predate my birth. As I review your stories, I realize they are much like my parents' stories. Now you are all free in a new home. I guess you can never prejudge what life will bring.

I also wrote down how you gained your freedom in Missouri and worked your way west as a cook on a wagon train. I'm sure you took precautions for your safety. But it must have taken courage to set out alone. My father says that your life speaks of courage and commitment. From starting your laundry business in Colorado to helping ex-slaves make their way west, you have been prepared to face every challenge. I am proud to have met you.

Your loving nephew,
Thomas

Clara Brown

Prefixes *re-* and *pre-*

Activity One

About Prefix

A prefix is a word part added to the beginning of a root word to make a new word. The prefix *re-* usually means "back" or "again." *Return* means "to go back" or "come or happen again." The prefix *pre-* means "before." *Preschool* means "before the age of going to regular school." Knowing the meanings of common prefixes helps you read and understand unfamiliar words. As your teacher reads *Aunt Clara Brown*, listen for the prefixes *re-* or *pre-* at the beginning of words.

Prefix in Context

With a partner, read *Aunt Clara Brown* to find words with the prefixes *re-* or *pre-*. Write the words in a chart like the one below. Then, use your understanding of prefixes to write the definition of each word.

WORDS WITH PREFIX *RE-*	DEFINITION
rebuild	to build again

Activity Two

Explore Words Together

Look at the list of the words on the right. Add the prefix *re-* and/or *pre-* to each word to make a new word. Take turns with a partner, saying each new word and giving its meaning.

payment	heat
set	paint
write	gain

Activity Three

Cooking Pot

Explore Words in Writing

Write a paragraph about a time when you performed an act of kindness for someone. Include at least four words with the prefixes *re-* or *pre-* in your paragraph. Share your writing with a partner.

CATHERINE HAUN'S

Journey Across the Plains, 1849

retold by Myka-Lynne Sokoloff

The Gold Rush of 1849 drew a quarter of a million people to Northern California. Some people were seeking adventure. Many were escaping debt. They hoped to strike it rich and rebuild their lives. Catherine Haun and her husband were among this latter group. Catherine Haun's memories of their journey offer a picture of daily life on the way west. This is her story.

Leaving Home

In January 1849, we thought of traveling to California. We longed to pick up enough gold to return home and repay our debts. Our party consisted of six men and two women. It included my husband Mr. Haun, my brother Derrick, Mr. Bowen, and myself. Three young men would act as drivers and a woman would cook for us all. Mr. Haun was chosen to lead our group.

We were all expected to lend a hand. This could mean building campfires and washing dishes. It also could mean protecting each other from danger. Men and women alike might be called on to restrain a loaded wagon on a downgrade or lift it over boulders as we climbed a mountain.

> How does the introduction help you learn about the author's purpose?

We filled two wagons with items we hoped to sell at fabulous prices. Surely, those in the "land of gold" would buy or barter for our goods. The idea was a fine one, but we never got the goods over the first mountain. Flour and bacon filled a third wagon. A fourth wagon carried additional supplies. We carried dried meat, dried fruit and vegetables and a few pots and pans, as well as two boards that would serve as a table. The wagon also held some bedding and a tent. For a luxury, we carried a gallon each of wild plum and crabapple preserves and blackberry jam.

I packed a dark wool dress, which served me constantly throughout the journey. The wool protected me from the sun and the winds. It had the advantage of needing little washing. We had few washday supplies and often had to carry water from miles away. I also packed an apron and a kerchief. It was three months before we were thoroughly ready. Finally, on April 24, 1849, we left our home in Clinton, Iowa.

What do you know about Catherine Haun from reading this page?

On Our Way

We covered only ten miles the first day, as both man and beast were fatigued. I recall that I woke the next morning almost dazed with dread at the thought of the adventure ahead of us. At that point, the woman who had agreed to cook for us decided not to go on. I surprised us all by offering to do the cooking, knowing others would help.

After a month of travel, we had crossed only the state of Iowa. A quick glance at a survey map showed that we had gone about 350 miles. Every mile was beautifully green and well watered. We joined a larger party before crossing the Missouri River. It was a tedious crossing. We took the wheels off the wagons. We piled the wagon beds with goods and then covered them with canvas to keep everything dry. We tied ropes to the animals' horns or necks, so the current would not carry them away. We reassembled the wagons on the other side. We had to inspect them to make sure everything was back in its proper place. In this manner, it took a week for the entire group to cross.

Why might the author give so much detail about the river crossing?

Buffalo

This was the land of the buffalo. One day, a herd came in our direction like a black cloud. The threatening mountain advanced with wild snorts, noses almost to the ground, and tails flying in midair. When buffalo stampede, they do not retreat or change course for anything. Some of our wagons were in their way and were destroyed, but fortunately, no one was killed.

Two of the buffalo supplied us with fresh meat. Later, we buried the leg bone in coals of dried buffalo chips and ate the marrow, or inside of the bone. I have never tasted such rich, delicious food! One family preserved some of the meat and made jerky. Later, when rations were low, our precautions came in handy. The jerked meat was all dried up and dusty. But when one stares hunger in the face, one isn't particular about trifles like a little dust.

Why do you think the author included the details about the buffalo?

Dried buffalo chips were very useful as fuel. When we had no wood on the barren plain, we carried empty bags and picked up chips. We could hardly have gotten along without this useful animal.

Reaching California

We finally reached Sacramento, California, on November 4, 1849. It was just six months and ten days since we had left our starting point in Iowa. We were all in pretty good condition. We went on to Marysville in January. There were only a half dozen houses, all at very high prices. My husband resorted to drawing up a will and charging $150.00. This seemed to be a lucky sign. We gave up all thought of hunting for gold, and he hung out a sign as a lawyer. After 2,400 miles and nine months of living in a tent, we were glad to settle down. We prepared for our new life.

Why do you think authors write about journeys?

Think and Respond

Reflect and Write

• You and your partner have read sections of *Catherine Haun's Journey Across the Plains, 1849*. Discuss with a partner the summary of your section and the inferences you made.

• For each section you read, write on one side of an index card the author's purpose for writing that section. On the other side of the index card write the details in the text that led you to that inference. Then find another set of partners and compare information.

Prefixes in Context

Reread the journal to find examples of words with the prefixes *re-* and *pre-*. Then work with a partner to write a letter in Catherine Haun's voice describing the journey. Include the words in the letter.

Turn and Talk
INFER: AUTHOR'S PURPOSE

Discuss with a partner what you have learned so far about how to infer an author's purpose.

• What does "author's purpose" mean? How do you infer an author's purpose?

Review the events in *Catherine Haun's Journey Across the Plains, 1849* with a partner. Then, with your partner, make an inference about the author's purpose for the entire selection.

Critical Thinking

With a group, brainstorm a list of reasons why people might move to a new place. Return to *Catherine Haun's Journey Across the Plains, 1849*, and write the reasons the Hauns traveled west. Discuss these questions together.

• How do you know the Hauns changed their plans and stayed in California?

• Which events on the journey do you think Catherine Haun found most and least enjoyable? Explain your choices.

My Life on the Homestead

Dear Diary,

1880

Father and Brother love it here on the **homestead**. They have long dreamed of moving west to Colorado. You can see the joy in their eyes when they and the infrequent visitor **inspect** the map that outlines our land. My father has hung the map on the wall like a fine work of art from a museum back East.

I shouldn't complain—Father and Brother have worked hard to build a secure place for us to live. Money has been tight, and many times I've watched them **barter** for the essential items they could not afford to buy. Both are proud of what they have accomplished.

I'm proud of them, too, but I long for the city. This is no **existence** for a girl of 16. I want other girls and women to talk to—I want the excitement of Denver! Sometimes at night I dream that I hear the whistle of a **locomotive** that has come to take me from this place. One day, Diary, when I am old enough I promise I'll catch a real train and flee my life on the homestead.

Alice

Structured Vocabulary Discussion

Work with a partner to review all of your vocabulary words. Then classify as many words as you can into two categories: nouns and verbs. When you are finished, share your lists with the class. Some words may fit into more than one category.

Throughout the week, add to your vocabulary journal entries. Record new insights and other words that relate to this week's vocabulary.

Picture It

Copy this word web into your vocabulary journal. Fill in the circles with things that people can **inspect**.

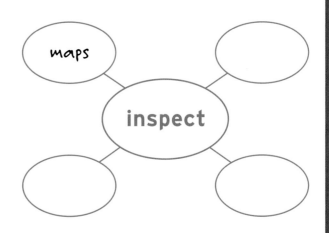

maps

inspect

Copy this word organizer into your vocabulary journal. Fill in the boxes with descriptions of a **homestead**.

homestead

a new place to live

King of the West

by Ann Weil

Here we come,
a million tons of iron and steel,
powered by coal and steam,
stronger than countless horses,
faster than a shooting star,
thundering west—all the way to the setting sun.

The locomotive
is King of the West
The leader of all
that is to come,
thundering west—all the way to the setting sun.

New towns spring up
as we pass each station.
Where once were grass and buffalo,
are now farms and shops,
thundering west—all the way to the setting sun.

The whistle blows
louder than dynamite.
Twin tracks finally meeting
at the horizon,
thundering west—all the way to the setting sun.

THE PONY EXPRESS

The Pony Express didn't last long. It started in April 1860, and closed down in October 1861. That's only 18 months. The Civil War and the transcontinental telegraph put an end to its glory. But the Pony Express's feats inspired many movies. It's still alive in our minds.

Here Comes the Mail!

The Pony Express carried mail between Sacramento, California, and St. Joseph, Missouri. That's a distance of nearly 2,000 miles. The average letter made the trip in 10 days. That isn't a bad record! The fastest trip was 7 days, 17 hours. Those riders carried a speech by President Abraham Lincoln. The country was on the edge of war. The riders didn't want to keep people waiting for news.

Another Kind of Relay!

A good relay system made fast trips possible for the Pony Express. The 190 stations along the route were spaced about 10 to 12 miles apart. Each rider rode from 35 to 70 miles before handing the mail to the next rider. That's quite a distance if you're riding as fast as you can!

Monument to the Pony Express Rider: Julesburg, Colorado

Contractions

Activity One

About Contractions

A contraction is a shortening of one or two words into one word by replacing some of the letters with an apostrophe. *Can't*, for instance, is the contraction for *cannot*. The *n* and *o* in not have been replaced by the apostrophe. As your teacher reads *The Pony Express*, listen for words that are contractions.

Contractions in Context

With a partner, read *The Pony Express*. Find the contractions and list them in a chart like the one below. Then indicate what word or words are being contracted.

CONTRACTION	FIRST WORD	SECOND WORD
that's	that	is

Activity Two

Explore Words Together

With a partner, look at the list of words on the right. Take turns forming a contraction for each combination of words.

I am	who is
we are	they have
let us	they will

Activity Three

Explore Words in Writing

Write five sentences about the Pony Express, using at least one contraction in each sentence. You can use the contractions from Activity One and Activity Two or think of additional contractions. Exchange your sentences with a partner and tell each other what words form the contractions.

One Hundred Sixty Miles of
Bad Weather!

by Melissa Blackwell Burke

As people settled the West, they needed to communicate with those in the East. Mail was the only way to get news back and forth. But there were few mail carriers, and the system was slow. In 1860, some businessmen organized a relay system of horses and riders to deliver mail. They traveled across the country in just ten days. Back then, that was a very short period of time. The system was known as the Pony Express. Young men on fast horses faced long hours in the saddle and a sometimes brutal existence. But they always got the mail through. Some riders were as young as 11. Most were no older than 17.

The Pony Express grabbed the attention of the nation. The riders captured the true spirit of the West. The following story is a work of fiction. But it's based on details from writings and interviews with real Pony Express riders. Some of them said that winter was the worst enemy a Pony Express rider could face.

What information do you learn from an introduction that is different from the information that you learn from an adventure story?

Part of the ad read "young, skinny fellows with expert riding skills wanted. Must be prepared to face danger daily." When Abe Stark answered the ad, he knew that he would be perfect for the Pony Express. At 15, he was young, all right, and his older brothers always teased him about how thin he was. More than anything else, Abe felt that he was born to ride horses. The folks at the Pony Express office apparently didn't disagree, because they hired him to put the mail through.

That's how on a January morning, Abe found himself standing next to a saddled horse waiting for a Pony Express rider. One galloped alongside Abe's horse and swung the mailbag over. Abe mounted the horse and rode hard into a howling blizzard. The snow was already piled in drifts three feet high. A biting cold wind whipped fiercely at both Abe and the horse. Abe knew he had 75 miles to ride before turning the mail over to the next rider. He said to himself, "No turning back."

What comparisons can you make between Abe and heroes in other adventure stories?

For hours, Abe and his horse battled the snowstorm across the flat and wide-open plains of Nebraska. For both horse and rider, there was nothing to do but wallow through and move ahead. Abe was more concerned about the horse than he was about himself, and he whispered to the animal, "You can do this. You're as tough as nails, just like me. You're young and strong like me, too, so on we go!"

Does the setting of this story remind you of the setting in other things you have seen or read about? Explain.

The last few miles near Fort Kearney dragged slowly and Abe was relieved when he finally had the station in sight. As he got closer, he could make out a saddled horse ready to go. When he was almost upon it, the stationmaster stepped outside. "The rider here's sick, so you'll have to ride on," he shouted into the wind.

Once a rider started out, he couldn't stop until he got the mail to the next station. If there was no rider to replace him there, then he had to ride on. Every Pony Express rider understood these things very clearly. No matter the weather, no matter what happened along the route, the mail had to go through.

How is Abe's experience at this station similar to and different from his experience at other stations along the route?

Abe grabbed the bag and mounted the fresh horse. "It's 32 miles to the next station," he said to himself. "A hundred miles isn't much of a long ride." And it wouldn't have been a particularly long ride if it hadn't been for the wild weather. The blizzard had become blinding and it was impossible for Abe to tell where the road was. A few times, Abe slid off the horse, walked around to find the road, and then remounted the horse. Finally, Abe realized that the best thing to do was to lead the horse back and forth until daylight came and he could see the road again.

As soon as daylight broke, Abe set out in search of the station. He found it, along with a breakfast that seemed to revive him a bit. When Abe asked the stationmaster where the next rider was, the man answered with silence and a stare. With a nod, Abe got on another fresh horse to ride another 25 miles to the next station. He recalled giving his word of honor to put the mail through, and he knew that's what he had to do.

Abe had been riding for more then 24 hours in a raging blizzard that seemed to only be getting worse. He could feel the temperature dropping. And the road was almost impassable with snow. In order to make any progress, Abe had to get off his horse, stamp down the snow, and lead the horse through.

Finally, he made it to Big Sandy. Only there was no rider waiting for him there, either. When the stationmaster heard what Abe had been through, he agreed to ride the mail. He'd gotten only about a mile down the road when the rider meant to relieve Abe caught up and took over for the stationmaster.

What connections can you make between Abe at the beginning of the story and at the end?

Back at the station, Abe had already fallen fast asleep on a cot. He slept for nine straight hours. When he woke up, he recounted to the stationmaster, "I dreamed I was back on my parents' homestead helping to build a barn. Then a rider galloped up and tossed me a mailbag. I suppose I'm ready to ride for the Pony Express again."

Think and Respond

Reflect and Write

- You and your partner have read sections of *One Hundred Sixty Miles of Bad Weather!* and shared your thoughts about the text. Discuss how each thought relates to the text.

- On one side of an index card, write one connection you could make between the story and your experience. On the other side of the index card, write how your experience is similar to or different from the information in the story.

Contractions in Context

Reread *One Hundred Sixty Miles of Bad Weather!* to find examples of contractions. Then work with a partner to use contractions in creating a short newspaper story about Abe's heroic effort. Share your newspaper story with the class.

Turn and Talk

MAKE CONNECTIONS: COMPARE/CONTRAST INFORMATION

Discuss with a partner what you have learned so far about how to compare and contrast information.

- How can you make connections by comparing and contrasting information?

- How does comparing and contrasting information help you become a better reader?

Review the connections you made for *One Hundred Sixty Miles of Bad Weather!* Discuss with a partner how making connections by comparing and contrasting information helped you understand the story better.

Critical Thinking

With a partner, write a list of the reasons Abe continued to travel during the storm. Then discuss these questions together.

- Why do you think people like Abe are so dedicated to their jobs?

- How does Abe exhibit the traits of a good Pony Express rider?

- Do you think Abe would be willing to make such a ride again? Explain your answer.

Spring Skiing, 2002
Rob Gonsalves (1959–present)

Viewing

The artist who painted this picture is Rob Gonsalves. He paints pictures inspired by dreams and imagination. Many of his paintings fool the eye.

1. What do you see in the picture that looks real? What in the picture is not real?

2. In what way does the painting show the laws of gravity? In what ways does the painting ignore the laws of gravity?

3. What does the title *Spring Skiing* mean to the people in the world of this painting? What does the title mean to you?

In This UNIT

In this unit, you will read about the force of gravity on objects. You will also explore how force and friction affect athletes and their equipment.

Contents

Modeled Reading

Shared Reading

Interactive Reading

What Goes Up Must Come Down

MIRETTE ON THE HIGH WIRE

written and illustrated by
Emily Arnold McCully

Critical Listening

Critical listening means listening to
compare and contrast the ideas and
characters in a selection. Listen to the focus
questions your teacher will read to you.

IN DEFENSE OF PLANET EARTH

In Defense of Planet Earth brings the League of Titans to the big screen. As the movie opens, these popular comic-strip heroes answer the call to save Earth. Invaders from another world are poised to take over Planet Earth. From start to finish, the Titans never **waver** in their sense of duty.

As every kid knows, the Titans have many powers. But their most amazing power is the ability to overcome **gravity**. They do so with a variety of devices, including special boots and belts. So equipped, the Titans are a **force** to be reckoned with. They give the aliens something to remember.

In Defense of Planet Earth contains many terrific special effects. One of the best scenes is a fierce conflict on a high wire. The foes face off high above a city street in a dance that is both terrifying and **comical** at the same time. The high-wire scene alone is worth the price of admission. The entire action-packed movie will be hard for anyone to **resist**.

comical   force   gravity   resist   waver

Structured Vocabulary Discussion

Work with a partner or in a small group to fill in the following blanks. Be sure you can explain how the words are related.

Wet is to *dry* as *serious* is to _____.

Divide is to *separate* as _____ is to *oppose*.

Strength is to *force* as _____ is to *hesitate*.

Throughout the week, add to your vocabulary journal entries. Record new insights and other words that relate to this week's vocabulary.

Picture It

Copy this word organizer into your vocabulary journal. Fill in the boxes with examples of the effect that the **force** of **gravity** has on objects.

force of gravity

causes an apple to fall from a tree

Copy this word web into your vocabulary journal. Fill in the circles with ways you can **waver**.

change mind

waver

LUCIE TO THE RESCUE

Ask Questions

Visuals

Many selections you read include pictures, charts, graphs, diagrams, or other visuals. As you read such selections, ask questions about how the visuals are related to the text. Do the visuals help explain or extend the information in the text? Asking questions about visuals will help you better understand what you read.

Questions about VISUALS can help you understand how they relate to the text.

Ask questions about visuals in order to learn more information and to understand how they enhance the text.

TURN AND TALK Listen to your teacher read the following lines from *Mirette on the High Wire*. Study the picture at the bottom of page 323. Then discuss with a partner the following questions.

- What details in the poster help explain the text?

- What details in the poster provide information that is not in the text?

Bellini stepped out onto the wire and saluted the crowd. He took a step and then froze. The crowd cheered wildly. But something was wrong. Mirette knew at once what it was. For a moment she was as frozen as Bellini was.

Then she threw herself at the door behind her, ran inside, up flight after flight of stairs, and out through a skylight to the roof.

She stretched her hands to Bellini. He smiled and began to walk toward her. She stepped onto the wire, and with the most intense pleasure, as she had always imagined it might be, she started to cross the sky.

TAKE IT WITH YOU Remember to ask questions about visuals as you read other selections. Use a chart like the one below to help you understand how visuals are related to the text.

Preview the text and place a ✔ next to the type of visual you find.

☑ **Illustration** ☑ **Chart** ☑ **Time Line**
☑ **Photograph** ☑ **Map** ☑ **Graph**

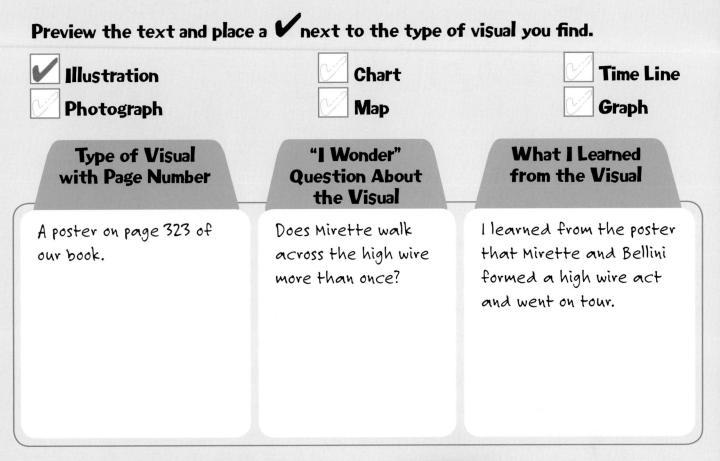

Type of Visual with Page Number	"I Wonder" Question About the Visual	What I Learned from the Visual
A poster on page 323 of our book.	Does Mirette walk across the high wire more than once?	I learned from the poster that Mirette and Bellini formed a high wire act and went on tour.

WHAT COMES DOWN

by Jeanie Stewart

Mrs. Estes started our gravity lesson with a question. "If Galileo dropped weights of 8 lb and 15 lb off the Leaning Tower of Pisa, which would hit the ground first?" Everyone shouted that the heavier weight would hit first. Instead of telling us if we were right, Mrs. Estes sent Simon, Claire, and me outside to do experiments. Simon climbed the steps to a raised platform with a bag of items. Claire put on safety glasses and sat on the ground below him. I stood nearby and recorded our findings.

People in Galileo's time believed that objects of different weights fell at different speeds. Galileo disagreed. He said all objects fall at the same rate. It is air resistance that sometimes makes them land at different times. Legend holds that Galileo offered proof. He dropped different-sized cannonballs off the Leaning Tower of Pisa. They landed at the same time. He was right!

Experiment 1   11:15 a.m.

Simon held a metal ball weighing 1 lb in one hand and a rubber ball weighing 8 oz in his other. With his arms straight out, approximately 8 ft from the ground, he dropped both items at the same time. Even though the 1 lb ball was twice as heavy, it hit the ground at the same time as the 8 oz ball.

Experiment 2   11:20 a.m.

Simon dropped a ping-pong ball and a golf ball. From a height of 5 ft, the ping-pong ball and the golf ball landed at the same time.

Experiment 3   11:25 a.m.

Simon dropped the golf ball and a round rock about the size of the golf ball from the platform, 5 ft above the ground. The rock and the golf ball hit the ground together.

We returned to the classroom. Mrs. Estes asked us to report our findings. When we finished, we stated our conclusion: Gravity will pull objects toward Earth at the same speed regardless of weight. The students were surprised when they realized their prediction was wrong.

NASA has conducted one of Galileo's falling-objects experiments on the Moon. Galileo claimed that, in the absence of air resistance, a feather and stone would drop at the same rate. What better place to see if he was right than on the Moon, where there is no air? Apollo 15 astronaut David Scott dropped a feather and a hammer. Galileo was right! Both objects hit the ground at the same time.

What It's Like to Weigh NOTHING

Dear Mary Jess,

I hear you want to be an astronaut when you grow up. I thought you might like to hear what I got to do yrs. ago. In college, I was part of NASA's Reduced Gravity Student Flight Opportunities Program. The program lets students conduct zero-wt experiments on a NASA plane.

The plane flies in a series of arcs called parabolas for a couple of hrs. The top of each parabola is about 30,000 ft high. As the plane passes the top of the arc, you become weightless. You stay weightless for about 25 sec on each arc.

I weigh 160 lb on the ground. It's kind of amazing to think that I dropped from 160 lbs to 0 lb in less than a minute.

If you get a chance to apply for the Reduced Gravity program when you're in college, don't hesitate. Being weightless is a once-in-a-lifetime opportunity. Hold onto your dream, M. J.— it is a terrific one.

Love,

Uncle T. J.

Abbreviations

Activity One

About Abbreviations

An abbreviation is a shortened form of a word or a phrase. Most abbreviations contain letters from the original word or words and are followed by periods. For example, the word *year* is abbreviated as *yr*. The abbreviations for most measurements are not followed by a period. For example, *ft* is the abbreviation for *feet*. A few abbreviations use one or more letters that are not in the original word. The word *pound*, for instance, is abbreviated as *lb*. As your teacher reads *What It's Like to Weigh Nothing*, follow along and look for common abbreviations.

Abbreviations in Context

With a partner, read *What It's Like to Weigh Nothing* to find abbreviations. Write the abbreviations in a chart like the one below. Then, write the full word that each abbreviation represents.

ABBREVIATIONS	WORD
yrs.	years

Activity Two

Explore Words Together

Look at the list of the words on the right. Take turns with a partner stating the correct abbreviation for each word.

apartment	pint
November	Doctor
mile	ounce

Activity Three

Explore Words in Writing

Use at least four abbreviations from Activity One and Activity Two in a paragraph about weightlessness. Share your paragraph with a partner.

How GRAVITY WAS INVENTED

by Kathleen Powell

On Earth long ago, before buildings and cars and even people, things were very different from the way they are now. This was a time before gravity. Since Earth had no pull, anything loose would just float away. Rivers and streams were all underground where the water couldn't escape. The only water above ground was in ice-covered lakes or oceans. The fish constantly complained about bumping their heads on the 3 yds of ice. Even air had to hold onto Earth like glue. Birds and flying insects had to be strong indeed to fly through the sticky stuff.

It wasn't bad for trees and grass. They had very deep roots, and clay dirt was so gummy that it stuck to Earth. But animals had to hang on for dear life. They devised clever ways to keep from drifting into space. Elephant attempted to glue his feet to the ground, but he accidentally glued his trunk instead. He stretched it terribly trying to unstick it. Tiger tried to grow roots on the end of his paws in order to claw into the ground, like the trees, but he wasn't very successful. (This is why elephants today have such long noses and tigers have long claws!)

What does it mean that "Earth had no pull"? How do the visuals show you the meaning?

332

Can you tell from the illustration why the monkey's ropes are not a good, long-term solution to the lack of gravity?

Ms. Monkey, who was good with her hands, created a profitable business weaving long strands of rope. Animals could attach one end to a tree and the other end to themselves and float happily for hours at a high elevation. "Ropes for sale!" Ms. Monkey would shout. "All lengths and thicknesses! Here's a nice rope for you, Gopher; it's 100 ft long," she might say, or, "Perhaps a strong one—50 mm thick for you, Hippo?"

Most animals lived in underground caves where they floated securely about. Trolls ruled this underground world. Now, you may have heard about trolls who are ugly and cruel. But the trolls of long-ago Earth were not like that at all! They were gentle and wise and attractive, with purple eyes, pointy green hair, and stumpy legs. Everyone respected the trolls—especially the wise King Troll.

So this is how things were in the long-ago time, and for many years, the animals were fairly content. But as time went by, the animals grew more restless. Just like you and I get tired of staying indoors on rainy days, the underground animals longed to live in sunshine. But how could they?

Spider was the kindest animal of all. Although she could easily hold onto the ground, she saw how miserable Elephant and Tiger and the others were. "We must find a way to help," she announced to Dr. Silkworm one day. Now Dr. Silkworm felt fortunate, being one of the few animals living above ground. He loved quiet walks in the P.M. Additional animals on land would just make things noisy. But after a brief hesitation, he agreed to help.

Day after day, Spider and Dr. Silkworm looked for an appropriate solution. They tried this, and then that, but nothing worked. Then one day, as Dr. Silkworm munched idly on a mulberry leaf, he watched Spider weave a web to catch a snack. Dr. Silkworm suddenly shouted, "I've got it! Come on!" And Dr. Silkworm hurried Spider to a comfortable cave where he sat down and started weaving. At first Spider thought Dr. Silkworm was making a cocoon, as silkworms often do. But then, "Look!" explained Dr. Silkworm. "I've created a lump!" And so he had—he had woven silk around thick, gooey clay until it was transformed into an extremely hard, sticky rock.

How is the illustration on this page related to the text?

334

Spider wasn't entirely impressed, but she wanted to be polite. "What an absolutely magnificent sticky lump! But I don't see how will it help."

Dr. Silkworm explained excitedly, "Silk attracts the clay. If we weave enough lumps, things will attract each other."

"Yes," agreed Spider, doubtfully, "but the Earth is 12,000 mi across! Is this possible?"

This was not a question for a common spider and silkworm. "We should ask King Troll," suggested Dr. Silkworm. So Spider and Dr. Silkworm crawled along the chain of caves until they arrived at the magnificent home of King Troll.

"Please, Sir. We know how to make things attract each other," explained Dr. Silkworm respectfully. And he gave the king a brief description of how weaving might benefit the animals.

The wise King Troll wasn't convinced. Other animals had come before with notions about increasing Earth's stickiness. After hearing Dr. Silkworm's story, he floated around, thinking. He was so deep in thought that he hardly noticed when he bumped his head (again) on the cave ceiling. But the bump made him consider what it would be like to stand on a hard surface.

"If the other animals agree," announced King Troll, "I think you should try!"

What information do you learn from the illustrations on this page?

Spider and Dr. Silkworm were overjoyed! But much work lay ahead. They spread the word that animals everywhere should weave clay into lumps. Everyone set to work. The spiders and silkworms of the world could barely provide enough silk. Before long, sticky rocks were everywhere!

But as you know, things on Earth change. Spring changes to summer, tadpoles change into frogs, etc. And so it was on long-ago Earth that things began to change. Rocks began sticking to each other, and gradually even the air's stickiness was pulled into the rocks. Birds commented upon how clear the air was at their high elevation.

One day, Rabbit exclaimed, "Look at that! The shape of my foot is in the dirt!" The animals had never seen footprints before. Another day, Bear grumbled, "Hmmm . . . my paws feel a bit heavy today." Eventually, after not-too-many years, everything was attracted to Earth. The Earth had gravity at last!

So the next time you walk—and not float—across a room, recall this version of how gravity came to be. And if you notice a spider or silkworm, be sure to say, "Thank you!"

What questions can you write about the illustrations in this story?

Think and Respond

Reflect and Write

• You and your partner took turns reading *How Gravity Was Invented* and writing two words. Discuss with your partner your words and thoughts.

• On one side of an index card, write down one question that you asked yourself when you saw an illustration. On the other side, write how the visual helped you answer the question.

Abbreviations in Context

Reread *How Gravity Was Invented* to find examples of abbreviations. Then work with a partner to write a thank-you note the animals may have written to Spider and Dr. Silkworm. Include at least four abbreviations in the note.

Turn and Talk

ASK QUESTIONS: VISUALS

Discuss with a partner what you have learned so far about how to ask questions concerning the use of visuals.

• How can asking questions about visuals help you understand what you read?

With your partner, determine whether the illustrations in *How Gravity Was Invented* explain information in the text or provide additional information.

Critical Thinking

In a small group, discuss why gravity is important. Write a list of things that gravity affects. Look back at *How Gravity Was Invented*. Discuss how the various characters in the story tried to live in a world without gravity. Then discuss answers to these questions.

• How did the various characters in the story try to deal with the lack of gravity on Earth?

• Would a scientist explain gravity the same way that this story explains it? Why or why not?

Lose 100 Pounds OVERNIGHT!

Want to lose weight instantly? I have the answer—**release** yourself from Earth's gravity by moving to another planet. Even though this is not possible, let's explore what would happen to your weight if you could actually move to some other distant planet.

Consider the following **brief** explanation. Weight is the effect of gravity on mass. Mass is the quantity of matter that an object contains. On other planets, your mass would stay the same, but your weight would vary considerably. On a planet bigger than Earth, you would weigh more. But on the Moon or a smaller planet, you would weigh less. So let's **accelerate** out to a few other places in the solar system and **calculate** body weights.

The Moon has about one-sixth the gravity of Earth. So, if you weigh 120 pounds on Earth, you would weigh about 20 pounds on the Moon. Maybe that's a little too light. On Venus, with just over 90 percent of Earth's gravity, you would weigh 109 pounds. Does that sound better? But don't go to giant Jupiter. You're not going to like the results. There, you would experience a hefty **elevation** in weight to 304 pounds!

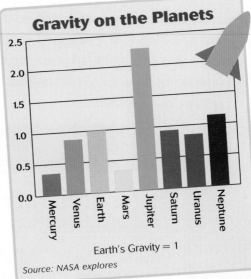

Gravity on the Planets

Mercury · Venus · Earth · Mars · Jupiter · Saturn · Uranus · Neptune

Earth's Gravity = 1

Source: NASA explores

Structured Vocabulary Discussion

When your teacher says a vocabulary word, you and your partner write on a sheet of paper the first words you think of. When your teacher says, "Stop," exchange papers with your partner and explain to each other the words on your lists.

Throughout the week, add to your vocabulary journal entries. Record new insights and other words that relate to this week's vocabulary.

Picture It

Copy this word wheel into your vocabulary journal. Name things you would want to **release**.

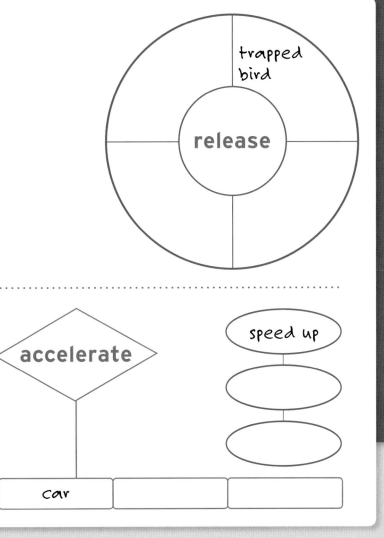

Copy this word organizer into your vocabulary journal. Fill in the ovals with words that mean **accelerate**. List in the boxes examples of things that can accelerate.

WALKING in SPACE

by Ann Weil

Rockets release me from gravity's pull.

I become weightless and start to fly.

Outside the window, I can see

A beautiful blue marble in the sky.

Our spacecraft lands on alien land.

My emotions surge till I almost cry.

That's when I realize how much I love

That beautiful blue marble in the sky.

My feet touch ground that is not my own.

I watch a shooting star zip by.

I am so far away from home.

My beautiful blue marble in the sky.

I take a step, then two, then three.
The time goes quickly by.
I look up to see a mist encircle
The beautiful blue marble in the sky.

I ask myself, how can this be?
Our planet seems vulnerable and shy,
Everyone should see Earth as I do now,
Our beautiful blue marble in the sky.

THE ORBITAL EXPRESS
TIPS FOR ZERO GRAVITY

Welcome aboard The Orbital Express! When we reach orbit, you will be weightless. Scientists often refer to this as zero gravity. But, as they will explain, an orbiting spaceship is still bound by Earth's gravity. The ship, and everything in it, is in free-fall around the planet. Got that? If not, don't worry. All you need to know is that in free-fall, everything floats around inside the ship.

We have ways to counteract weightlessness. You will be issued special shoes with gripping soles. They will give your feet "sticking power," enabling them to stay attached to the carpeting. Your flight attendant will also issue you a crash helmet. Please pay attention to him or her. Wear your helmet!

He or she will also be serving you a somewhat unusual meal. On The Orbital Express, we must serve semi-liquid food that you drink with a straw from a sealed tray. Enjoy your ride!

Pronouns

Activity One

About Pronouns

A pronoun is a word that takes the place of one or more nouns. People use pronouns to avoid repeating nouns. For example, *she* or *her* are pronouns that can be used in place of a proper name, such as *Mary*. Likewise, a group of people can be referred to as *they* or *them*, and an object can be called *it*. As your teacher reads *The Orbital Express*, listen for pronouns.

Pronouns in Context

With a partner, read *The Orbital Express*. Write each pronoun in a chart like the one below. Then explain what each pronoun stands for. Keep in mind that the same pronoun can refer to different nouns in different sentences.

PRONOUN	WHAT IT STANDS FOR
we	the people on The Orbital Express

Activity Two

Explore Words Together

With a partner, look at the list of words on the right. Discuss what pronoun or pronouns you could substitute for each word or group of words. Take turns creating sentences using the correct pronouns.

John

you and a friend

Lisa, Jeff, and Tony

a group of people

an object in the road

a collection of CDs

Activity Three

Explore Words in Writing

Select a paragraph in a favorite book. Rewrite the paragraph using as many pronouns as you can without changing the meaning of the paragraph. Exchange paragraphs, with a partner and see if you can replace the pronouns in your partner's paragraph with the appropriate nouns.

ADMIT ONE

AN OUT-OF-THIS-WORLD VACATION

by Alice Leonhardt

Forget camping at Yellowstone National Park. Forget visiting a theme park or two weeks at the beach. Even forget trips to beautiful spots around the world. The summer vacation of the future will be 60 miles straight up—into space.

Does this sound too "far out" to happen soon? Guess again. In 2001, the first space tourist, Dennis Tito, orbited Earth for ten days. His destination was the International Space Station (ISS). Since then, other people have also made the trip.

Some people think private citizens going into space for pleasure is a waste of time and money. I disagree. I believe space tourism has a bright future. Space tourism makes good business sense. Some companies are willing to put money into building the industry. Some private citizens will pay for the chance to go into space. Space tourism also makes good scientific sense. It will increase people's interest in space exploration. It will also help develop new tools for use in space. These tools will help advance space exploration.

The mothership takes off from a runway, carrying a small spaceplane.

What is the author's purpose in writing about space tourism?

The mothership carries the spaceplane up to an altitude of about 44,000 feet. The spaceplane detaches and fires its rocket engine.

The spaceplane flies up to an altitude of about 370,000 feet, or about 70 miles—the edge of space.

The spaceplane glides back and lands like a conventional airplane.

Race to Space

Private companies are racing to build and launch spacecraft. They hope these craft will carry large groups of people. One company is developing a craft that will take off like an airplane. Rocket engines will accelerate the craft to Mach 4 (four times the speed of sound). Then the craft will coast to an altitude of 62 miles. That's quite a ride!

Another company is building a craft that is carried into the air by a "mothership." In this design, the small spaceplane is attached to a larger airplane for takeoff. Once the large plane has reached a high altitude, it will release the spaceplane, which will then rocket into space. Both companies promise their passengers several minutes in space. During that time, they will experience weightlessness and view Earth.

What else does the future hold? Several companies are interested in building space hotels. If spaceplanes can carry tourists into space, why not give them a destination? Even some of the major hotel chains are thinking about space. These companies see the future. They believe in space tourism.

Why do you think the author includes information about building hotels in space?

Partner Jigsaw Technique Read a section of the article with a partner and write what you think the author's purpose was for that section. Be prepared to summarize your section and share ideas about the author's purpose.

The Cost of Space Travel

These companies should believe in space tourism. There are eager customers out there. Some did not even wait for the spacecraft to be finished before signing up. These people paid $200,000 each for a future flight. Granted, $200,000 is pricey. However, it is much less than the $20 million that Dennis Tito paid for his trip.

People involved in space tourism calculate that prices will continue to come down. Eric Anderson is the president of Space Adventures. That is the company that put Dennis Tito in space. Anderson thinks that everyone will be able to afford space travel in 50 years. Perhaps not everyone will be able to travel in space. However, I do think interest will grow. Some predict space tourists will number 15,000 each year by 2021. By then, Anderson believes, people will have colonized the Moon. It could become the first outer space hot spot. Fly to the Moon! Now *that's* a vacation!

Why did the author include the numbers and facts on this page?

Investing in Space Travel

Businesses and customers are not the only people who believe that space tourism is important. Congress seems to think so, too. In 2004 Congress passed a bill to help the new industry. The law is the Commercial Space Launch Amendments Act. This law makes it easier for businesses to invest in space travel. The return could be huge. One recent study says that space tourism could be a $1 billion-a-year business by 2021. Space flight is also risky. That is why the law prevents passengers from suing the government. Space tourism companies are required to warn customers of the danger. Early airplane travel was a bit wild. But it got safer. I think space travel will, too.

NASA does not seem to share this positive view. It puts very little budget money toward public space travel. Because space tourism will grow, those who doubt its importance will be won over. NASA and the public will see how the industry can benefit space exploration.

Why does the author point out that NASA is cautious about space tourism?

Let's Get Serious

Space tourism is in its pioneering phase. Prices are high and services are few. But as the demand for travel increases, companies will compete for travelers. They will lower prices. They will increase services. This will fuel the "space business." The adventurous will find jobs in space. And the increased revenue from tourism will fund future technology for exploring and developing the resources in space.

Business has always played a major role in moving this country forward. It is time for business to take the lead in space tourism. We must take space tourism seriously. If we do, we can open space travel to anyone who has ever dreamed of a vacation to the Moon and beyond.

Do the arguments the author presents match the author's purpose? Explain.

Think and Respond

Reflect and Write

- You and your partner have read a section of *An Out-of-This-World Vacation* and discussed your inference about the author's purpose. Discuss your ideas.

- On one side of an index card, write the author's purpose for the section you read. On the other side, write what details helped you infer the author's purpose. Find another partner team that read a different section and exchange information.

Pronouns in Context

Reread *An Out-of-This-World Vacation* to find examples of pronouns. Then, write a paragraph summarizing your view of space tourism. Be sure to include at least four pronouns in your paragraph. Share your paragraph with the class.

Turn and Talk

INFER: AUTHOR'S PURPOSE

Discuss with a partner what you have learned so far about how to infer the author's purpose.

- How can you figure out an author's purpose?

Review with a partner what you read about space travel in *An Out-of-This-World Vacation*. Then, with your partner, discuss how the author's purpose helped you understand space tourism.

Critical Thinking

With a partner, brainstorm reasons that people might want to travel in space. Review *An Out-of-This-World Vacation*. Then, discuss these questions.

- What arguments does the author present in support of her view?

- Did the author do a good job of using facts to support her opinion?

- Did the author persuade you to accept her view of space tourism? Why or why not?

The Science of Sports

Contents

Modeled Reading

Shared Reading

Interactive Reading

AMERICA'S CHAMPION SWIMMER

GERTRUDE EDERLE

By David A. Adler

Illustrated by Terry Widener

Appreciative Listening

Appreciative listening means listening for language that helps you create a picture in your mind. Listen to the focus questions your teacher will read to you.

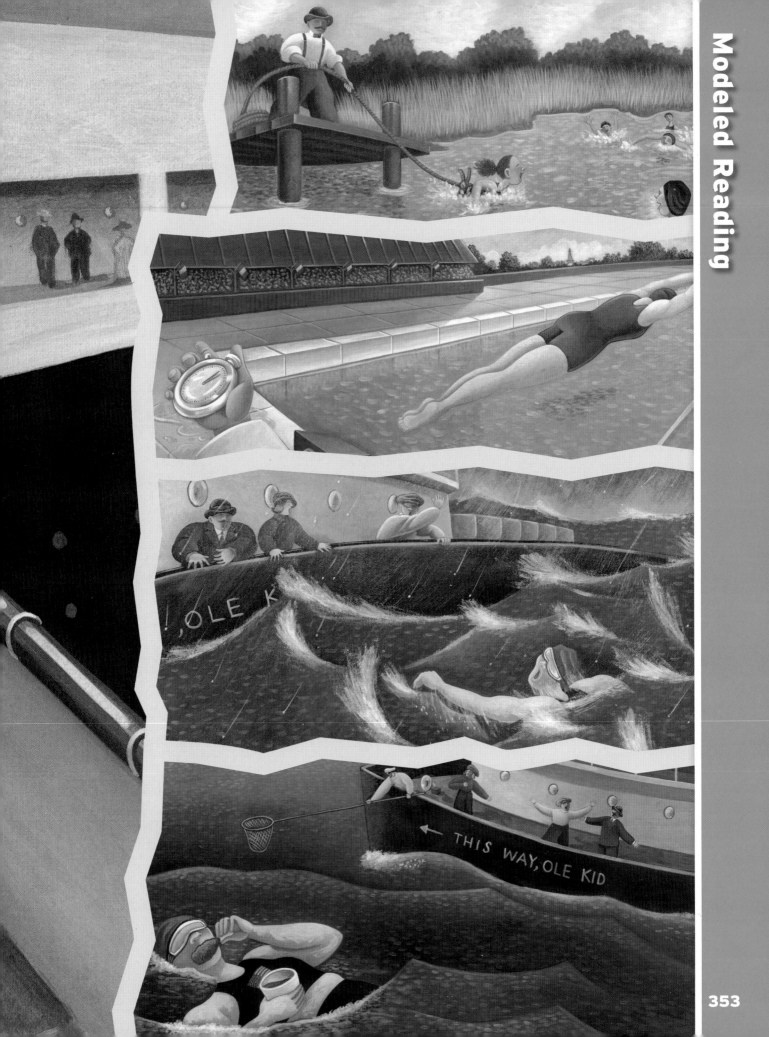

Rough Waters

Dear Sarita,

I just had to write to you about my latest project. I'm sure you'll think I'm crazy, but I've decided to make an **attempt** to swim the English Channel.

I imagine your jaw has dropped, but it's really not such an insane idea. I prefer to think of it as **courageous**. I'm not the greatest **athlete** in the world, but I think I can do this. I **estimate** that if I train hard for a year, I can get into good enough shape to make the 21-mile crossing.

I am a bit worried about what effect the force and **friction** of the waves will have on me. But consider Gertrude Ederle. She was the first woman to swim the channel, in 1926. Ederle (it's pronounced EH-der-lee) died in 2003 at the ripe old age of 97. So maybe that channel swim strengthened her.

Anyway, wish me luck.

Love,
Aunt Rosa

English Channel

Structured Vocabulary Discussion

Work with a partner or in a small group to fill in the following blanks. Be sure you can explain how the words are related.

Exit is to *leave* as _____ is to *try*.

Train is to _____ as *practice* is to *musician*.

Throughout the week, add to your vocabulary journal entries. Record new insights and other words that relate to this week's vocabulary.

Picture It

Copy this word web into your vocabulary journal. Fill in the circles with people who are **courageous**.

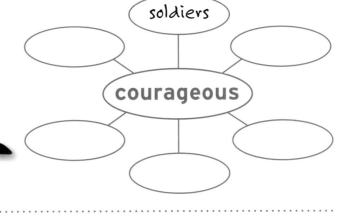

soldiers

courageous

Copy this word organizer into your vocabulary journal. Fill in the boxes with actions that can cause **friction**.

friction

rubbing my hands together

Determine Importance

Rank Information

Not all information in a selection is of equal importance. Some details are essential to your understanding. Other details are not essential. Ranking information will enable you to focus on important details and disregard those that are not important.

When you RANK INFORMATION, you decide how important it is.

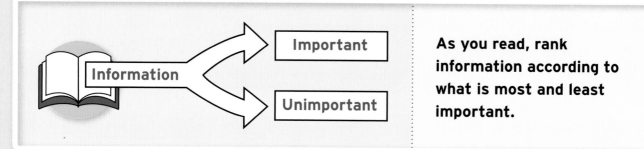

As you read, rank information according to what is most and least important.

TURN AND TALK Listen as your teacher reads the following lines from *America's Champion Swimmer: Gertrude Ederle*. With a partner, read the lines and choose the most important and unimportant details. Discuss the following questions.

• What details do you need to understand the passage?

• What details are not important?

Trudy did not give up her dream. She found a new trainer, and a year later, on Friday, August 6, she was ready to try again.

Trudy wore a red bathing cap and a two-piece bathing suit and goggles that she and her sister Margaret had designed. To protect her from the icy cold water, Margaret coated Trudy with lanolin and heavy grease. The greasing took a long time—too long for Trudy. "For heaven's sake," she complained. "Let's get started."

Finally, at a little past seven in the morning, she stepped into the water.

TAKE IT WITH YOU Focusing on what is important makes you a better reader. As you read other selections, determine the importance of information. Use a chart like this one to classify information. Rank information from 1 (most important) to 5 (least important). Focus more attention on the important information.

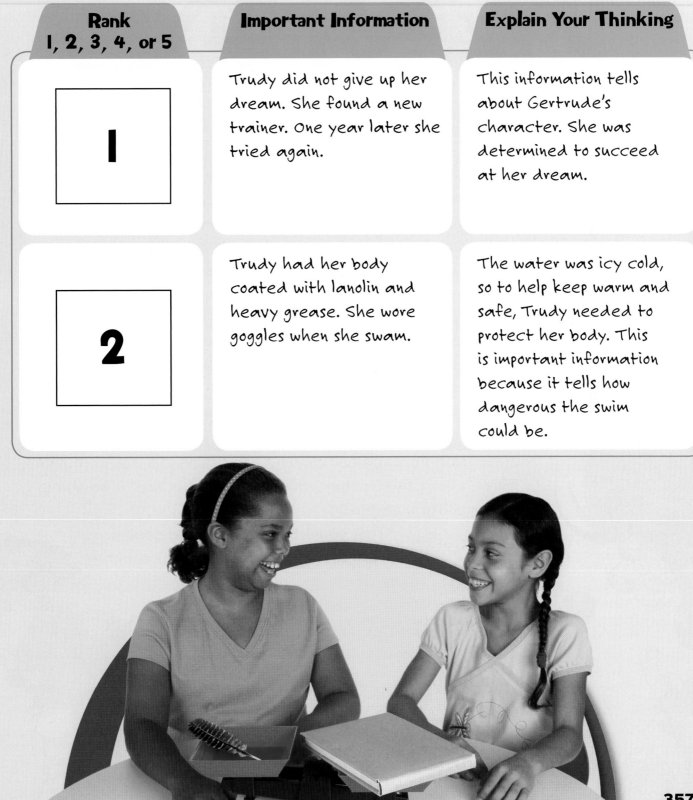

Rank 1, 2, 3, 4, or 5	Important Information	Explain Your Thinking
1	Trudy did not give up her dream. She found a new trainer. One year later she tried again.	This information tells about Gertrude's character. She was determined to succeed at her dream.
2	Trudy had her body coated with lanolin and heavy grease. She wore goggles when she swam.	The water was icy cold, so to help keep warm and safe, Trudy needed to protect her body. This is important information because it tells how dangerous the swim could be.

EXTREME Dogboarding

by Karen Lowther

Chay spun the hand-cast wheels of his new skateboard lightly as he and his dog Chulo approached the skateboard park. Chulo wagged his tail enthusiastically and jumped up to lick Chay's face. "Easy, easy," Chay laughed. "I think you're as eager as I am to get started!" Chay examined the hard rock maple deck of the skateboard he had received for his birthday. "First, we've got some things to learn. I don't want to bite off more than I can chew on my first day—falling on my face would be embarrassing, especially with an audience!"

Chay plopped on the grass beside Chulo and fastened his helmet and adjusted his elbow pads and kneepads, trying not to look foolish. "I'm not a fish out of water," he said, even though he felt a bit like one. As he fastened his wrist guards, Chay studied some of the other kids as they performed tricks on the skateboard ramps and half pipes. Chay watched a boy complete a fakie. "Look Chulo," Chay whispered. "Some day I'll be going backwards like that, too."

"That could be accomplished sooner than you think," said a voice behind him. Chay whipped around and saw his neighbor Megan standing behind him.

"Let me show you a few easy-as-pie tricks. First, I'll show you an ollie—the most basic skateboarding trick," said Megan. Chay watched intently as Megan's back foot smacked the rear end of the skateboard against the concrete while her front foot pulled the skateboard up into the air. When it was Chay's turn, he flipped the skateboard completely over. The second time Chay's foot hit the back end of the skateboard so hard he lost his balance and toppled to the ground. By the fourth try, Chay's move was perfection.

"See, I told you—it's like falling off a log. You're a natural," exclaimed Megan, looking truly impressed. Chay felt like a million dollars. He put down his skateboard, and he and Megan headed for the water fountain.

Just then Chulo let out a loud yelp. Megan and Chay spun around just in time to witness Chulo leaping onto the back of Chay's skateboard. Seconds later, the front of the skateboard arced into the air. A startled Chulo and the skateboard flew over a ramp, bit the dust, and landed safely.

"I can't believe it—now that really is extreme skateboarding!" shouted Megan. "Chulo did an ollie! I think the little guy just invented dogboarding." Chay laughed and hugged Chulo tightly around the neck.

Game Day

Feb. 21

Dear Diary,

Pam is really nervous about the game tomorrow. She's feeling dizzy and has butterflies in her stomach. You'd think she was scheduled to play in the NBA! I tried to tell her it's just the first game in the after-school basketball league. But she flew off the handle and said I wasn't being properly sympathetic.

I won't beat around the bush, Diary. Even though Pam is absolutely my best friend in the whole wide world, I think she is making way too much of this. It really goes against the grain for me to get this worked up over something that is supposed to be fun. I think she really needs to lighten up.

I really did try to be encouraging, but I don't think she wants to calm down. I think she enjoys making a mountain out of a molehill, as my dad would say. Pam even predicted that she's going to pass out on the basketball court from anxiety. But I told her that I am taking that forecast with a grain of salt.

Tish

Idioms

About Idioms

An idiom is an expression that does not mean what it says literally. For example, *face the music* means to accept responsibility for your actions. Idioms make it possible to say things in different ways. As your teacher reads *Game Day*, listen for idioms.

Idioms in Context

With a partner, read *Game Day*. Notice how the idioms are used to express ideas. Write down each idiom you find in a chart like the one below. Then work with your partner to explain what each idiom means.

IDIOM	DEFINITION
butterflies in her stomach	nervousness

Activity **Two**

Explore Words Together

Look at the list of idioms on the right. With a partner, research what each idiom means. Then discuss ways that you could use it.

fly the coop	pain in the neck
step on it	have a blast
raise the roof	as the crow flies

Activity **Three**

Explore Words in Writing

Choose three of the idioms from Activity Two. Use them in a paragraph about some recent activity you were involved in. You might write about a summer vacation trip or a day in school. Make sure the idioms work well together. Share your paragraph with a partner.

FAMOUS *Firsts*

by Ernestine Giesecke

*H*ave you ever wanted to be first at sports? You know— a blue-ribbon winner . . . top dog . . . the champ? Jackie Robinson, Roger Bannister, Althea Gibson, Junko Tabei, and Kristi Yamaguchi were firsts. Here are their stories.

JACKIE ROBINSON *First African American in the Major Leagues* Jackie Robinson played sports during his college days. He took part in baseball, football, basketball, and tennis. He ran track and field, and he swam. After serving in the army, Robinson played in the Negro American League. It was the only baseball league open to men of color.

Joining the Dodgers In 1946, Robinson joined the Brooklyn Dodgers. He became the first African American to play baseball in the Major Leagues. Robinson's first game was opening day of the 1947 season. He faced the Boston Braves. He also faced a hostile crowd. He was a fish out of water.

Breaking the Color Line Robinson hung in. He was an excellent athlete—fast and skillful. His courage and talent paid off. He was named Rookie of the Year. Robinson's actions helped break the game's "color line." His life is an inspiration to athletes as well as sports fans.

What would you rank as the most important information on this page? How did you make your decision?

Jackie Robinson

ROGER BANNISTER *First to Break the Four-Minute Mile* Many people thought running a mile in four minutes was not possible. Roger Bannister did not agree. He believed the four-minute mile barrier was a mental barrier, not a physical one. Bannister set out to prove he was right.

The Role of Oxygen Bannister was a medical student. He knew how muscles work. He knew that muscles need oxygen to move. The human body can put out little more than ten seconds of effort without oxygen.

> What information about Roger Bannister is the most important to help you understand how he reached his goal?

Bannister believed that good oxygen use was one key to reaching his goal. Pacing was the answer. An even pace would let Bannister mix effort that required oxygen with effort that did not.

The Role of Training Bannister thought another key was training. He believed that by slow, steady training he could improve his running time by two or three seconds each year. Bannister trained only 45 minutes a day. Most runners trained two to three hours a day.

On May 6, 1954, Bannister ran a mile in 3 minutes, 59 and four-tenths seconds. His prize was in the bag. Within two years, 16 other runners also broke the barrier.

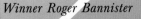

Winner Roger Bannister

Read, Cover, Remember, Retell Technique
With a partner, take turns reading as much text as you can cover with your hand. Then cover up what you read and retell the information to your partner.

ALTHEA GIBSON *First African American Wimbledon Champion* As a teen, Althea Gibson was long, lean, and very strong. Her road to fame began in the paddle tennis games arranged by the Police Athletic League. Gibson found she had a natural talent for hitting the ball. What's more, she loved to compete.

From the Paddle to the Racket In tennis, Gibson relied on her strong serve. She played boldly. And, at one inch under six feet, she could cover the whole court with ease. She soon dominated the games sponsored by the mostly black American Tennis Association.

Wimbledon At the time, racism was common in many sports. But Gibson's skill could not be denied. The U.S. National Championships asked her to play. Then, Wimbledon invited her to their courts. In 1957, like a bolt from the blue, Gibson won the women's singles and doubles at Wimbledon. Her win was the first for an African American man or woman.

How do the headings and subheadings on this page help you determine what information is important about Althea Gibson?

Wimbledon Trophy

Althea Gibson

364

JUNKO TABEI *First Woman to Reach the Top of Mt. Everest* A teacher introduced Junko Tabei to mountain climbing when she was ten years old. The young girl fell in love with the mountains and with climbing. Tabei could climb at her own pace, never feeling as though she had to win a race.

An All-Women Team When she was 30, Tabei read that two companies were planning an all-women climb of Mt. Everest. She applied at once. Tabei was a seasoned climber. Thus, she was picked to lead the group of 15.

Junko Tabei

Conquering Mt. Everest The women trained for three years before beginning the actual climb. Then, partway up the mountain, an avalanche buried the climbers' camp. Once everyone was accounted for, Tabei pressed on, playing it by ear. The bruised team inched its way to the top, sometimes crawling on hands and knees. Tabei reached the top on May 16, 1975. She was the first woman ever to do so.

> What clues can you use to figure out important and unimportant information about Junko Tabei's climb?

ROUTE UP MT. EVEREST

Summit
29,028 ft

Camp 4
26,000 ft

Camp 3
24,500 ft

Camp 2
21,300 ft

Camp 1
19,900 ft

Base Camp
19,900 ft

KRISTI YAMAGUCHI

First Asian American Woman to Win Olympic Gold As a child, Kristi Yamaguchi wore corrective casts. She had special shoes designed to reshape her feet. Kristi started skating to help strengthen her legs. Then she saw Dorothy Hamill win the 1976 Olympics. Kristi began to dream of winning her own gold medal.

What information would you rank as important on this page? What information would you rank as unimportant? Why?

Practice, Practice, Practice With that dream in mind, Kristi skated for hours every day before school. Kristi's physical stamina began to increase as a consequence of her skating after school, too. She began to excel at both singles and pairs skating. Eventually Kristi was forced to choose between singles and pairs. She chose singles and set to work to improve her artistry. She made her free skate program more imaginative.

Going for the Gold Kristi put her best foot forward and earned a place on the 1992 U.S. Olympic team. During the competition, Dorothy Hamill stopped by. She wished Kristi luck. With Dorothy's words ringing in her ears, Kristi took to the ice. Her skating earned her a gold medal. She became the first Asian American woman to win Olympic gold in any sport.

Kristi Yamaguchi

Olympic Gold Medal

Think and Respond

Reflect and Write

- You and your partner took turns retelling sections of *Famous Firsts*. Discuss with a partner what you retold to one another.

- On one side of an index card, write down the title of the section you read and its most important information. On the other side, write why you chose the information as important.

Idioms in Context

Reread *Famous Firsts* to find examples of idioms. Then work with a partner to use the idioms to create a short poem about sports heroes. Share your poem with the class.

Turn and Talk

DETERMINE IMPORTANCE: RANK INFORMATION

Discuss with a partner what you have learned so far about how to rank information.

- What does it mean to rank information?

- How do you figure out what is important and unimportant information?

Review the details you recorded for *Famous Firsts* with a partner. Explain to your partner how you determined which details were important and how they should be ranked.

Critical Thinking

With a group, brainstorm a list of qualities that good athletes possess. Write them on the left side of a piece of paper. When you're finished, return to *Famous Firsts* and on the right side of the page write the names of the athletes featured in the article. Then write answers to these questions

- What qualities do these athletes share?

- What obstacles did the athletes overcome to achieve their goals?

- What lessons do you think the author was trying to teach with these stories?

The Science of Batting

Welcome to Major League Baseball! You're about to watch athletes of great **ability**. If you're new to big-league ball, let us tell you a bit about the central drama of the game. That's the battle between pitcher and batter.

When the pitcher flings the ball toward the plate, it can travel up to 100 miles per hour. As a **consequence**, the batter's **reaction** must be lightning fast. He has less than half a second to swing the bat before the ball whizzes past him.

Needless to say, the **movement** of the bat is extremely important. The bat must meet the ball squarely. If it's just a fraction of an inch too high or too low, the batter won't get that desired home run.

Not many players have the **physical** skills to become great hitters. In the showdown between pitcher and batter, the pitcher usually wins. But maybe today you'll see some homers!

Structured Vocabulary Discussion

When your teacher says a vocabulary word, have the people in your group take turns saying the first word they think of. Continue until your teacher says, "Stop." Then have the last person who said a word explain how his or her word is related to the vocabulary word.

Throughout the week, add to your vocabulary journal entries. Record new insights and other words that relate to this week's vocabulary.

Picture It

Copy this word organizer into your vocabulary journal. Fill in the ovals with words that describe **reaction,** and list examples of **reaction** in the boxes.

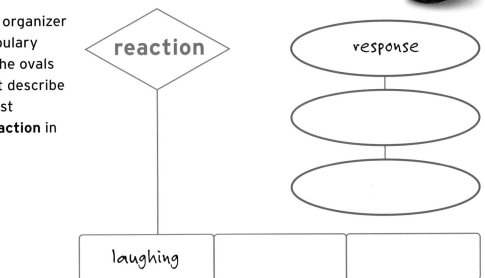

reaction

response

laughing

Copy this word wheel into your vocabulary journal. In the sections, name things that require **ability.**

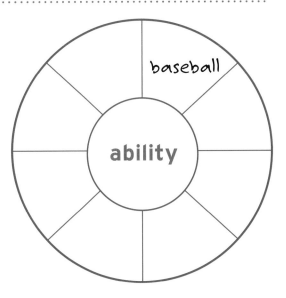

baseball

ability

The CYCLISTS' Song

by Ruth Siburt

Their tear-shaped helmets

Fasten under their chins

Their clothing hugs

Like second skins

The starter's gun cracks

And the movement begins.

Today,

Oh today

They'll conquer the wind.

Their bikes are the lightest
    Titanium steel
Their tires the fastest—
    Discs (not spokes) in the wheels

Their muscles the force
    That powers their rides
The cyclists leaning
    Converge
        D i v i d e

The blood in their bodies
    Thrums and sings—
      RACING!

The Paralympics

Racing

Every two years, the Paralympics swiftly follow the Olympics. Both games are held in the same city. The athletes who take part in the Paralympics share one thing in common. They all have physical challenges. The games started in 1948. Since then, they have steadily grown more popular. The games benefit more than just the athletes. They help audiences remember that anyone can play a sport.

Curling

In 2006, nearly 500 athletes took part in the winter games. Some of the sports of the winter games were skiing, curling, and even hockey. However, the summer games are even larger. Some 4,000 athletes usually compete. Of the many different events, swimming and sailing are popular. So are horseback riding and cycling. Judo also draws crowds there, as do team sports such as volleyball.

Basketball

One of the most exciting events is wheelchair basketball for both men and women. Team players are carefully chosen based on the rules and regulations for the game. The design of each wheelchair also must fall within narrowly defined limits.

Adverbs

Activity One

About Adverbs

An adverb is a word that describes a verb, an adjective, or another adverb. An adverb explains where, when, or how something happens. Many adverbs end in *ly*. But many do not. For example, if you say, "It rained *yesterday*," yesterday is an adverb. It tells when it rained. As your teacher reads *The Paralympics*, listen for adverbs.

Adverbs in Context

With a partner, read *The Paralympics* to find examples of adverbs. Write the adverbs in a chart like the one below. Then, tell what word it describes and whether it tells where, when, or how something happens.

ADVERB	WORD IT DESCRIBES	WHAT IT TELLS
usually	compete	when

Activity Two

Explore Words Together

With a partner, look at the list of adverbs on the right. Take turns using each adverb in a sentence. Have the person listening tell what word the adverb describes and what it tells about the word.

fairly	badly
suddenly	completely
often	courageously

Activity Three

Explore Words in Writing

Pick several of the adverbs from Activity One and Activity Two. Use them in writing a short paragraph about your favorite sport. Exchange paragraphs with a partner and circle the adverbs and underline the words they describe.

Curling

MANNY MASTERS
Curling

by Katie Sharp

Manny held his breath as he took his place at the hack. He bent his right leg and stretched the left behind him. Then he firmly grasped the red handle of the 42-pound granite stone. He was feeling intense pressure—this was the most important bonspiel, or curling competition, for 10- to 12-year-olds in the state.

Manny looked toward Pablo, the team's lead, standing inside the hog line at the other end of the rink. That line was the minimum distance Manny had to move the stone. On either side, Mark and Josh stood with brooms in hand, ready to sweep if needed.

Manny felt his heart pound hard inside his chest. Standing there ready to deliver his final stone, he couldn't believe how far he and his teammates had come. Just months ago, they had been slipping and sliding all over the ice. At one point, Manny almost called it quits.

What questions do you have about some of the terminology on this page? How could you find out the answers to your questions?

"I just don't think I have the ability to be a curler," he had told Pablo, Mark, and Josh at the time.

Curling Stone

"Come on, Manny," Pablo had replied to his friend's lack of confidence. "Remember when we first discovered curling during the Winter Olympics? We followed every match. You thought the sport was so awesome. We didn't know anything about curling, but we read all about it, learned the rules, and followed the best curlers in the world. You even made up your own curling competition. Remember trying to push hockey pucks on the sidewalk at the park?"

"Yeah," Mark had added, "those hockey pucks didn't move too well on the concrete."

Pablo had shot Mark a glance that told him he wasn't helping.

"But then Mr. Robinson saw us at the park," Pablo had continued, "and told us about the 'Come and Try Curling' event at the community center."

"I was the one who convinced Mr. Robinson to start the Kidz Curling classes," Manny had replied. "We were the first four to sign up."

"And it was your idea to start a team," Josh had added.

"I didn't know it was going to be so much work," Manny had said.

What questions do the illustrations and diagram on this page prompt you to ask?

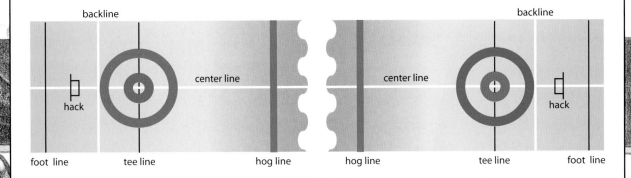

DIAGRAM OF A CURLING RINK

backline   center line   center line   backline

hack   hack

foot line   tee line   hog line   hog line   tee line   foot line

Pablo's pleading had convinced Manny to continue curling. Now here they were at their most important competition yet. And they were on the brink of making it to the championship event. The only thing that stood in their way was this delivery. Manny was about to deliver his team's eighth and final stone.

Manny again focused on Pablo across the rink. As the team captain, it was Pablo's job to tell Manny where to aim the stone. Pablo studied the 15 granite stones that had already been delivered. There were eight from the opponent and seven from their team. Pablo finally decided what Manny needed to do. He signaled to his teammate that he should deliver the stone to the left. Pablo had to use signals because he was more than 100 feet away from Manny.

Reverse Think-Aloud Technique
Listen as your partner reads part of the text aloud. Choose a point in the text to stop your partner and ask what he or she is thinking about the text at that moment. Then switch roles with your partner.

How does the illustration help express the importance of Pablo's studying the other stones?

Pablo hoped Manny's stone would knock out the opponent's stone that had landed to the left of the tee, or center, of the house. If he could do it, Manny's stone would be closest to the tee, winning the match. The team would qualify for the championship.

Pushing off the hack, Manny gracefully glided to the area just ahead of the hog line. If his feet passed the hog line, the other team would win. Manny pulled his arm back, then forward, and let go of the stone. As he did, he turned, or curled, it clockwise so it would travel left.

Pablo watched intently as the stone slid along the ice. He quickly realized it didn't have the speed to make it all the way to the tee.

"Sweep!" ordered Pablo, barking the command sharply.

Josh and Mark began sweeping their brooms back and forth in front of Manny's stone. Their action would help the stone move farther, increasing the chance that Pablo would get the reaction he wanted.

Why do you think the sweeping action would make the stone move farther?

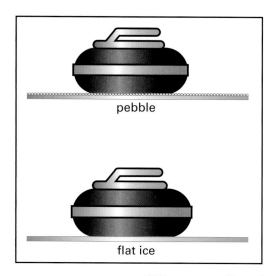

pebble

flat ice

As Manny watched them sweep, he recalled how Mr. Robinson had explained the fundamentals of curling.

"Water droplets are sprinkled on the ice. Frozen on contact, those droplets—called pebble—create a bumpy surface."

"Does that slow down the stone?" Manny had wanted to know.

"No, actually, the pebble enables the stone to travel more easily, because the stone comes in contact with less ice than it would if the surface were flat. Less contact means less friction between the stone and the ice. Also, the stone's weight melts the ice, creating a thin layer of water, which further reduces the friction."

"What does sweeping do?" Manny had asked.

"It changes the ice, further reducing the friction. Sweeping can add ten feet to a delivery!"

The crowd cheering brought Manny back to the present. His stone had pushed the opponent's stone away from the tee!

What questions do the illustrations of the curling stones help you answer?

Manny, Pablo, Josh, and Mark ran toward each other. All four slipped on the ice and slid into each other. As they laughed, they didn't care about the championship event. In this moment they already felt like champion curlers.

Think and Respond

Reflect and Write

- You and your partner took turns reading aloud *Manny Masters Curling* and asked questions about your thoughts. Discuss your questions and answers.

- On one side of an index card, write down the question that you thought of when you saw an illustration or diagram. On the other side, write down the answer to your question.

Adverbs in Context

Reread *Manny Masters Curling* to find examples of adverbs. Write down the words you find. Then include the words in a paragraph describing a fictional curling competition for your school newspaper. Share your description with a partner.

Turn and Talk

ASK QUESTIONS: VISUALS

Discuss with a partner what you have learned so far about asking questions about visuals.

- What are visuals?

- How do visuals help you make sense of what you read?

Choose one detail you listed about the curling rink diagram in *Manny Masters Curling*. Explain to a partner how that detail helped you understand the story or extend what you know about curling.

Critical Thinking

With a group, write down the roles force and friction play in the game of curling. Then write answers to these questions.

- Why do you think a sport like curling would take physical strength?

- Why do you think it would take a lot of practice to be good at curling?

- Why do you think it is important for the team captain to study the ice and the positions of the other stones before telling a player where to deliver a stone?

Route 6, Eastham, 1941
Edward Hopper (1882–1967)

UNIT: *Technology Matters!*

THEME **13** **Communication Revolution**

THEME **14** **Making Life Easier**

Viewing

The artist who painted this picture was Edward Hopper. Many of his paintings were pictures of city streets and lonely country roads.

1. What do you know about the painting from its title, *Route 6, Eastham, 1941*?

2. How is the word *communication* shown in the painting?

3. If the painter had included people in the painting, how would your reaction to the painting change?

4. What impact would cars and cell phones have on the details of the painting or on the people who live in this house?

In This UNIT

In this unit, you will read about the importance of technology. You will learn about advances in communications. You will also explore how inventions make life easier.

Contents

Communication Revolution

EDISON'S
Fantastic
PHONOGRAPH

by Diana Kimpton   illustrated by M. P. Robertson

Precise Listening

Precise listening means listening to understand characters. Listen to the focus questions your teacher will read to you.

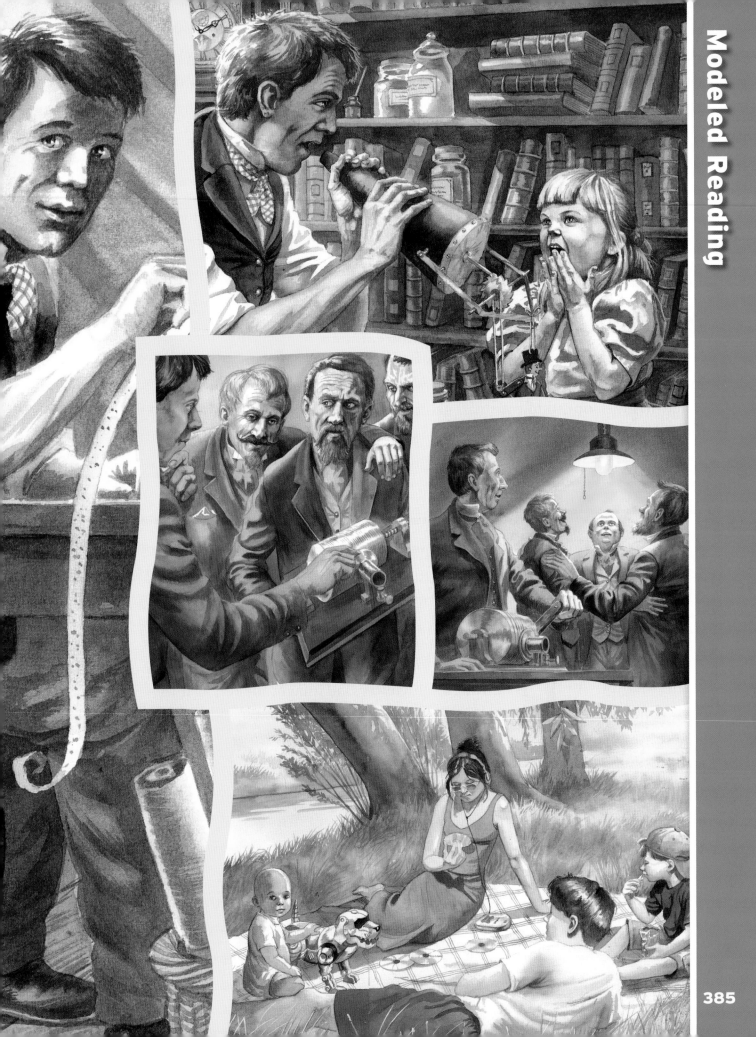

Vocabulary

The Birth of the Movies

Did You Know? Thomas Edison and his workers produced some of the earliest **machinery** for viewing moving pictures. Edison's first such machine—the kinetoscope—looked like a small cabinet. A person looked through a viewing hole on top to see a short movie. Most movies were about a minute long.

Edison's Kinetoscope

Kinetoscope mechanics

Did You Know? Edison's machine used a long strip of film wound around **cylinder** after cylinder. The strip contained a series of individual pictures. As the strip ran past a light in the machine, each picture flickered for less than a second. To the person looking through the viewer, the images looked as if they were moving. One of Edison's first movies showed one of his workers sneezing.

Did You Know? Edison knew that movies could become an important form of **commerce**. But first, Edison and his workers had to make **adjustments** to the invention to **improve** it. The result was a machine that could show a movie to a roomful of people!

Edison's theatre, Black Maria

Structured Vocabulary Discussion

Work with a partner to answer the following questions. Explain your answers.

Which is more likely to include a *cylinder*, a CD player or a CD?

Which is more likely to *improve* in the future, computers or pencil sharpeners?

Throughout the week, add to your vocabulary journal entries. Record new insights and other words that relate to this week's vocabulary.

Picture It

Copy this word wheel into your vocabulary journal. Fill in the sections with examples of **machinery**.

lawnmower

machinery

Filmstrip of a man sneezing for Thomas Edison's Kinetoscope; January 7, 1894

Copy this word organizer into your vocabulary journal. Fill in the boxes with examples of ways people could **improve** communcations.

improve

People could make communications faster.

Monitor Understanding

Reflect on Purpose

To identify what is important, reflect on your purpose for reading. Your purpose for reading can lead you to discover what part of the text is important.

Your **PURPOSE FOR READING** determines which parts of the text are most important to understand.

Strategies

When you don't understand, think about your purpose for reading to decide if that part of the text is important.

TURN AND TALK Listen to your teacher read the following lines from *Edison's Fantastic Phonograph*. With a partner, discuss what sections are important to your understanding. Then answer the following questions.

- What is your purpose for reading?

- How can your purpose for reading help you figure out what parts of the text are important?

[Edison said] "The sound of my voice made the needle move and the needle made a picture of the noise I made. Now let's see if I can turn that picture back into sound."

Nervously Edison made the final adjustments to the phonograph. The other men held their breath as he started to turn the handle. As the cylinder went round and round, the scratches on the tin foil made another needle move.

To everyone's amazement, they heard *Mary Had a Little Lamb* again. But this time Edison wasn't saying anything—the words were coming from the phonograph.

TAKE IT WITH YOU When you monitor your understanding, remember to reflect on your purpose for reading so that you can determine whether unclear sections are important. As you read other selections, use a chart like the one below to help you with the process.

Page Where I Noticed I Didn't Understand	What I Did						Which One Worked?
	Reread	Reflected On Purpose	Thought About Meaning	Asked Myself Questions	Thought About Strategies	Used Genre Knowledge	
The page where the cylinder went round and round and the scratches on the tin foil made the needle move.	✓	✔	✓	✓	✓	✓	Reflecting on my purpose helped me understand I was reading to learn historical information. I did not have to be able to picture the exact details of the science experiment.

Cast Your Vote for the Future!

Telegraph
Telephone
Television
Radio
Internet

by Sue Miller

Suppose I asked you to vote on the most important invention in the communications revolution. What would you pick? You have quite a few choices. The invention of the printing press revolutionized the world. What would we do without books and other printed material? The telegraph let people send messages across the country in an instant, but the telegraph's time has come and gone. The telephone and its little giant cousin—the cell phone—have had a dramatic impact on communications. Radio and television have brought us a world of information and entertainment. Each of these choices is worthy of your vote. However, if called on to choose the *most* dramatic, revolutionary invention, you should definitely pick the Internet.

Voting for the Internet is important for several reasons. First, it has come a long way in a short time. Most people heard of the Internet in the 1990s—not very long ago. Yet today, more than 70 percent of adults in the United States use the Internet. The rate is even higher among teenagers—around 87 percent. And the numbers keep growing.

Second, the Internet has many uses. People use e-mail and instant messaging to keep in touch. Many people go online to find information. Some get all their news online. Many people also look for information about things to buy. And growing numbers of people shop online. Many others go online for fun. Online games are popular. So are hobby sites. These many uses increase the value of the Internet.

Third, the Internet is "the future," as it gets faster and easier to use. And more people get a chance to use it. Today, you can get telephone service over the Internet. You can download music and videos. Some radio stations send their broadcast over the Internet. You can watch television programs and movies online. You can even control the temperature of your house and turn on your oven for dinner over the Internet. Many of these things were not possible ten or even five years ago. Can you even imagine what will be possible in another ten years?

What other choice among the inventions can offer as much? The Internet is popular. It has many uses. And it keeps getting better. Cast your vote for the Internet as the most important invention of the communications revolution!

How Often U.S. Teenagers Use the Internet

35% Weekly Use

14% Less Than Weekly

51% Daily Use

391

LET'S TALK

To: Grandma

From: Katie

Hi Grandma,

Greetings from the planet IM! I guess my last e-mail did seem like it was written in another language. I'm sorry that it seemed a bit confusing. Or, as we would say here on Instant Message, I'm :(my last e-mail left you :-/ and ^_^ and :-O. Allow me to translate: I'm sad my last e-mail left you confused and squinty eyed and surprised. I should have waited to use my language until I explained everything.

My language is not as difficult as all of the Chinese words you learned during your vacation last year. I know you can learn this language within minutes. Those little punctuation-mark symbols are called smileys or emoticons. You have to read most of them with your head tilted toward the left. After a few lessons, you will be lol (laughing out loud) at all of the neat things you can write. I can already see a :D (big smile) on your face.

:*) :*) (kiss, kiss), Katie

SUP

brb

Prepositions

Activity One

About Prepositions

A preposition is a word that relates a noun or pronoun to other words in a sentence. The noun or pronoun is called the object of the preposition. Examples of prepositions include *to*, *from*, *in*, *across*, *behind*, *above*, *around*, and *through*. A prepositional phrase is a group of words made up of the preposition, its object, and any words that come between the preposition and the object. As your teacher reads *Let's Talk*, listen for prepositions.

Prepositions in Context

Read *Let's Talk* and make a list of all the prepositional phrases. Write down each preposition and prepositional phrase in a table like the following. Then underline the object of the proposition in the phrase.

PREPOSITIONS	PREPOSITIONAL PHRASE
from	from the planet IM!

Activity Two

Explore Words Together

With a partner, takes turns using each of the prepositions listed at the right in a sentence that you speak aloud. Have the partner listening to the sentence indicate the object of the preposition.

below	except
beyond	under
through	between

Activity Three

Explore Words in Writing

Write a poem about e-mail or instant messaging using as many prepositions as you can. Exchange your poem with a partner and have the partner underline the prepositions and their objects.

AND AWAY WE GO

by David Dreier

Maria sat staring at the screen of her brand new laptop computer. Her mother was probably right—the hardest part of any project is getting started. Still, she thought, a report on virtual globes might be fun. Maria liked geography. She also loved her new computer. Her dad had said that doing research for her report would be a good way for Maria to check out the machine. Maria figured she shouldn't disagree. She had begged her parents for a laptop to replace her old computer, claiming it would be more convenient. Now it was time to put the computer's connection to the Internet to good use.

What is your purpose for reading this story?

Maria typed "virtual globes" into the search engine. She sighed when she saw the dozens of Web pages on the list. Some would probably be great, but which ones? It would take a while to check out each Web page. Maria decided to check her e-mail first. She had one new e-mail from her friend Kim. Kim's message was short: "I found a Web site that should help with your report. I think you'll be amazed!" Kim had included a link.

Maria started to get excited. Kim liked to be mysterious, but she was good at finding information on the Web. Maybe this site would be helpful. Anyway, it was worth a try. Maria clicked on the link.

Immediately a Web page with swirling galaxies appeared. At the top, in capital letters, was the word *VORTEX*. The only other words on the screen were the labels on two buttons: "Enter" and "Exit."

Do you need to understand what a vortex is to understand this story? Why or why not?

Maria hesitated for a second and then took a deep breath and clicked "Enter." Blackness, then a single question: "Do you believe in the infinite possibilities of time and space?" There were three possible answers: "Yes," "No," and "Maybe." Maria was about to choose "Maybe," but then thought better of it. She clicked "Yes."

A message flashed on the screen: "Congratulations. You have been accepted at Vortex." Next, the screen instructed Maria to type the location of any place on Earth into the box in the center of the screen and click the "Go" button.

"This is a strange site," Maria muttered. "Well, what's a good location? How about Grandma and Grandpa's house?" She typed in the street address of her grandparents' home in Chicago, Illinois, and clicked "Go."

Suddenly, the computer screen was like a window in a rocket streaking away from Earth. To her amazement, Maria could see her house and San Diego getting smaller and smaller. All of the state of California came in view. Within seconds, Maria was looking down on the whole country. Just as suddenly, the view raced downward toward Illinois. Maria saw Lake Michigan and then Chicago. Finally, streets appeared. A moment later, Maria zoomed toward the roof of her grandparents' house. The screen went dark.

"Wow, that was absolutely awesome!" Maria said, as she caught her breath.

What information on this page is important for your purpose for reading?

"Maria?!"

Maria glanced toward the voice, and gasped loudly. Her grandmother stood in the door. Confused, Maria looked around. She was no longer in her bedroom in California. Maria *really* was at her grandparents' house—the living room to be exact. "How did I get here?" Maria asked.

"That's just what I was going to ask you. Where are your mom and dad?" her grandmother said, looking every bit as confused as Maria.

Before Maria could answer, her grandfather walked in the room and looked at Maria in surprise.

"How did you get here?" her grandfather said. "I didn't know you were coming for a visit."

"Neither did I, Grandpa," was all Maria could manage to say.

"Where are your parents?" her grandfather asked, as he looked around for them, puzzled.

Maria tried to explain. She told her grandparents about the Vortex Web site and her virtual globe assignment. She even showed them her new computer. Her grandparents listened. But they clearly had their doubts about the story. Maria couldn't blame them. The story sounded unbelievable, even to her ears. But they also knew that Maria's parents wouldn't put her on a plane for Chicago without calling first. Desperate, Maria offered to prove that her story was true.

Why do you think Maria's grandparents doubted her story?

Maria's grandparents looked at one another, trying to decide what to do. Finally, her grandfather said, "How are you going to do that, my dear?"

"I'll type in another location and take you both with me. Where would you like to go?" Maria replied.

"Okay," her grandfather said. "I need a good waffle recipe for the cookbook I'm working on. So let's go to Belgium. They make really good waffles there. Your grandmother and I have been planning a trip to Brussels. Maybe you can save us the airfare." He looked at Maria's grandmother and winked. Fetching a guidebook, Maria's grandfather gave Maria the address of a restaurant in Brussels, Belgium, to type into the box on the Vortex Web page.

Is it important to your understanding of the story that you know the location of Brussels, Belgium? Why or why not?

Before Maria's grandfather had time to say, "Now that we know your laptop isn't a transport machine, I'm calling your parents," the three were whisked off to Belgium. Everyone agreed, the waffles were worth the wild ride!

Think and Respond

Reflect and Write

- You and your partner have shared your thoughts and ideas as you read the story. Discuss your ideas and choose two that help you understand the story best.

- On two index cards, write the information that is most important to understand. On the back of each card write how the information relates to your purpose for reading the story.

Prepositions in Context

Reread *And Away We Go* to find examples of prepositions. Work with a partner to see who can find the most prepositions. Then use some of the prepositions to write an introduction to your own fantasy about virtual globes. You may use additional prepositions. Exchange papers with a partner and circle each of the prepositions in your partner's introduction.

Turn and Talk

MONITOR UNDERSTANDING: REFLECT ON PURPOSE

Discuss with a partner what you have learned so far about monitoring understanding by reflecting on your purpose.

- What does it mean to reflect on your purpose?

- How do you determine whether information is important?

Choose one example of something that was unclear to you while reading *And Away We Go*. Explain to a partner how your purpose for reading helped you to monitor your understanding.

Critical Thinking

Talk about how the Vortex virtual globe was similar to and different from real virtual globes on the Internet. Then write answers to these questions.

- What do you think would happen if you searched for a specific address on a virtual globe Web site?

- What do you think the author wanted you to learn from the story?

The Communications Revolution

1837—Telegraph

Samuel Morse demonstrates his telegraph. The telegraph sends coded messages over electrical wires. The code is a series of long and short clicking sounds. The clicks represent different letters. This **convenient** system is called Morse code.

1876—Telephone

Alexander Graham Bell invents the phone. The phone uses electricity to send speech sounds. Soon people are talking over a **network** of phone lines.

1895—Radio

Guglielmo Marconi sends the first radio signal through the air. The wireless age is born. This leads to the invention of the modern radio. Later advances **assure** the success of radio.

1939—Television

Years of experimenting have produced an **efficient** way to send pictures and sound through the air. NBC starts airing TV shows on a regular basis. The television age is born.

1970s to 1990s—Computers and the Internet

Small, affordable computers hit the market. The computer age is born. The **Internet** soon connects these machines around the world.

Structured Vocabulary Discussion

Work with a partner to review all of your vocabulary words. Then classify as many words as you can into three categories: (1) noun, (2) verb, or (3) adjective. When you are finished, share your ideas with the class. Be sure to explain why you put each word in the category you did and whether any words fit into more than one category.

Throughout the week, add to your vocabulary journal entries. Record new insights and other words that relate to this week's vocabulary.

Picture It

Copy this word wheel into your vocabulary journal. Fill in the sections of the circle with the names of things that make life more **convenient**.

Marconi's first beam transmitter, 1895.

cell phones

convenient

Copy this word organizer into your vocabulary journal. Fill in the ovals with words that describe a network, and list examples of things that belong to a **network** in the boxes.

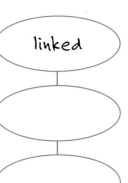

network

linked

computers

Take NASA's World Wind for a Spin

Where is a really good globe when you need one? Thanks to NASA and the Internet, right on your computer desktop. NASA's World Wind brings the world to you in amazing detail by linking to the network of information sources available on the Internet.

Zoom in for a closer look at the smoke produced by fires in California.

Control the globe's level of detail. Turn the lines of longitude and latitude and the country boundaries on or off. Tilt the globe in any angle. The names of places appear as you zoom in on the globe.

Look at a bird's-eye view of the streets and buildings in Washington, D.C.

Use the collection of satellite images and information. More details and place names appear as you zoom in on an area.

Track fires, floods, storms, dust, and smoke around the world. Navigate quickly using icons.

Compare different areas of the world. Which is hottest: Africa, Europe, or Asia? Use World Wind to answer this question.

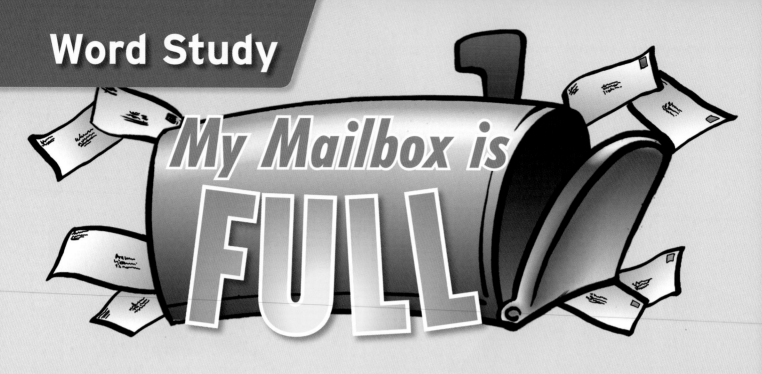

My Mailbox is FULL

E-mail's such a useful tool,
Remarkable in every way.
I just wish there was a rule
That spammers have to stay away.

Relentless in their money quest,
They send me scads of hopeful pitches,
With promises that I'll be blessed
With perfect health and endless riches.

It's pointless, though, to get uptight.
Just hit "delete," and by the score,
Those uncountable spams take flight.
But then—yikes!—here come some more.

Suffixes -*ful*, -*able*, and -*less*

Activity One

About Suffixes

A suffix is a word part added to the end of a root word that changes the word's meaning. These suffixes -*ful*, -*able*, and -*less* turn nouns and verbs into adjectives. You may have to change the spelling of the root word when you add a suffix. As your teacher reads *My Mailbox Is Full*, listen for words with the suffixes -*ful*, -*able*, and -*less*.

Suffixes in Context

Read *My Mailbox is Full* and make a list of all the adjectives with the suffixes -*ful*, -*able*, and -*less*. Create a chart like the one below. Write down each adjective, the adjective's meaning, the root word, and the root word's meaning. If the root word can be used as both a noun and a verb, give both meanings.

ADJECTIVE	MEANING	ROOT	MEANING
hopeful	full of hope	hope	(n.) a feeling that what you want to happen will happen (v.) to wish for something and expect it to happen

Activity Two

Explore Words Together

With a partner, think of as many words as you can that can be made into new words by adding the suffixes -*ful*, -*able*, and -*less*. Use the words listed at the right to get started.

care   joy

thought   enjoy

account   taste

Activity Three

Explore Words in Writing

Use some of the words with suffixes you created in Activity Two to write a paragraph about your favorite way of communicating with your friends. Exchange paragraphs with a partner and circle the suffixes in your partner's paragraph.

Delete

Tracking the Bird Flu

by Ann Weil

I got a call from a friend yesterday. She asked if I would help her son, Sam, with a research project using the Internet. Sam is in fifth grade, and he needed to do research on bird flu. I was happy to help. I'm a writer and use the Internet for research. The Internet can be an efficient way to find good reference materials. However, I know that researchers have to be careful when choosing Web sites. Not all information on the Internet is accurate or useful. I liked the idea of passing along a few pointers to Sam.

When Sam arrived, I asked him, "What do you know about bird flu?"

Sam said "Bird flu is another name for *avian influenza.*"

I suggested that first we should find a detailed definition. Sam needed to know a few specifics before he could decide what to focus on in his report. He sat down at the computer. Sam typed *bird flu* into the search engine while I looked over his shoulder.

Why does Sam need a definition of bird flu?

Needless to say, we got back a very long list of Web sites. "It'll take me hours to check all those sites!" Sam exclaimed.

"Don't worry, Sam," I said. "Using the Internet can feel a bit like looking for a needle in a haystack. Once you've had some practice, you'll learn ways to save time and go right for the good information."

I recognized a number of really helpful Web sites on the list. The Centers for Disease Control (CDC) and the World Health Organization (WHO) Web sites were near the top of the list. I told Sam that these were useful and trustworthy Web sites. The CDC is a U.S. government site and WHO is an organization that deals with health issues around the world. "Let's look at the World Health Organization Web site" I said. "I know that site has great maps showing the spread of bird flu.

"Wait, I still need a definition," said Sam. "What about something that gives an overall description of the problem—something like a newspaper or magazine Web site?" I agreed with Sam, so we scanned the list for good possibilities.

What information is important for you to understand on this page?

Sam spotted a news organization near the top of the list that looked like it would have what we were looking for. He clicked on that choice. The link took him to a page that listed all the organization's articles about bird flu. Sam chose one with the title "Q & A: Defining Bird Flu" and read the article.

Sam read aloud, "When bird flu occurs in wild birds, it is often harmless. Other birds, including chickens, are not so lucky. If these birds catch certain types of bird flu, they die in high numbers. The virus usually doesn't affect people. In 1997, however, 18 people in Hong Kong caught bird flu. Some of these people died. Scientists named the flu strain H5N1. A new outbreak of the virus occurred in people in 2003, first in Hong Kong and at the end of the year in Vietnam." The article noted that scientists have been careful to track the spread of bird flu as it slowly moves to other countries.

Say Something Technique Take turns reading a section of text, covering it up, and then saying something about it to your partner. You may say any thought or idea that the text brings to your mind.

Why would a map be a good way to show the spread of bird flu?

Number of Cases of Avian Flu

Vietnam

Indonesia

Thailand

China

Turkey

Cambodia

Sam said, "I think I've decided the topic for my report: tracking the bird flu. My teacher wants us to cite our sources. Our reports must include maps, graphs, charts, and pictures. Is that going to be a problem?"

"Don't worry," I said. "Some Internet sites display information in the form of visuals."

Sam still looked a little worried, however. He said "I'm curious just how fast and where the bird flu is spreading."

I suggested that we visit the World Health Organization Web site and take a look at the maps. Sam could see from the maps that most of the cases of bird flu in people had occurred in Asia. The largest number of cases in chickens and other birds had occurred in Asia, too. I told Sam that the spread of the virus among birds did not assure that lots of people would get sick. It was not that easy to pass the virus from birds to humans.

Is there any information on this page that is not important to your purpose for reading?

China

Vietnam

Laos

Thailand

Cambodia

I told Sam that the Internet is a remarkable way to get the word out about bird flu. The technology is also capable of collecting information. I did a quick search for an online article I'd read. The article explains that scientists are using satellites and radio transmitters to track wild birds. Scientists know that wild birds are spreading avian flu as they move around. This makes tracking the birds' movements important.

In what ways did Sam have to rank information as he did research for his report?

"Sam," I asked, "do you know what GPS is?"

"Yes," Sam answered. "It's an abbreviation for *global positioning system*. I've seen those on TV."

I explained that here in the United States, animal doctors are using handheld GPS units and satellite maps to mark the locations of chicken farms. This will make it easier to react quickly if bird flu ever reaches the United States. "That's pretty cool!" Sam answered. I thought about it for second and decided Sam was right. It is pretty cool!

Think and Respond

Reflect and Write

- As you read *Tracking the Bird Flu*, you and your partner have said something about every section you read. Discuss which of your ideas or thoughts gave important information from the selection.

- With your partner, write down four thoughts or ideas about the selection on index cards. Put one thought or idea on each index card. Then rank the cards according to importance.

Suffixes in Context

Reread *Tracking the Bird Flu* to find examples of the suffixes *-ful*, *-able*, and *-less*. Write down the words you find. Then use the words in four sentences about the bird flu. Exchange your favorite sentence with a partner and have your partner underline the suffixes.

Turn and Talk Review

DETERMINE IMPORTANCE: RANK INFORMATION

Discuss with a partner what you have learned so far about ranking information.

- How do you rank information in a selection?

- How does ranking information help you determine importance?

Examine the index cards you created for information in *Tracking the Bird Flu*. With another partner pair, discuss how you classified and ranked the information as important or unimportant and how this helped you understand the selection.

Critical Thinking

Discuss what the author tells you about how scientists track bird flu. Then answer each of these questions.

- How is bird flu different from most diseases in the way it is spread?

- How has the need to track bird flu required scientists to use new tools and methods?

- How might the use of the Internet make it easier to track the bird flu?

Contents

Making Life Easier

Queen of Inventions

How the Sewing Machine Changed the World

by Laurie Carlson

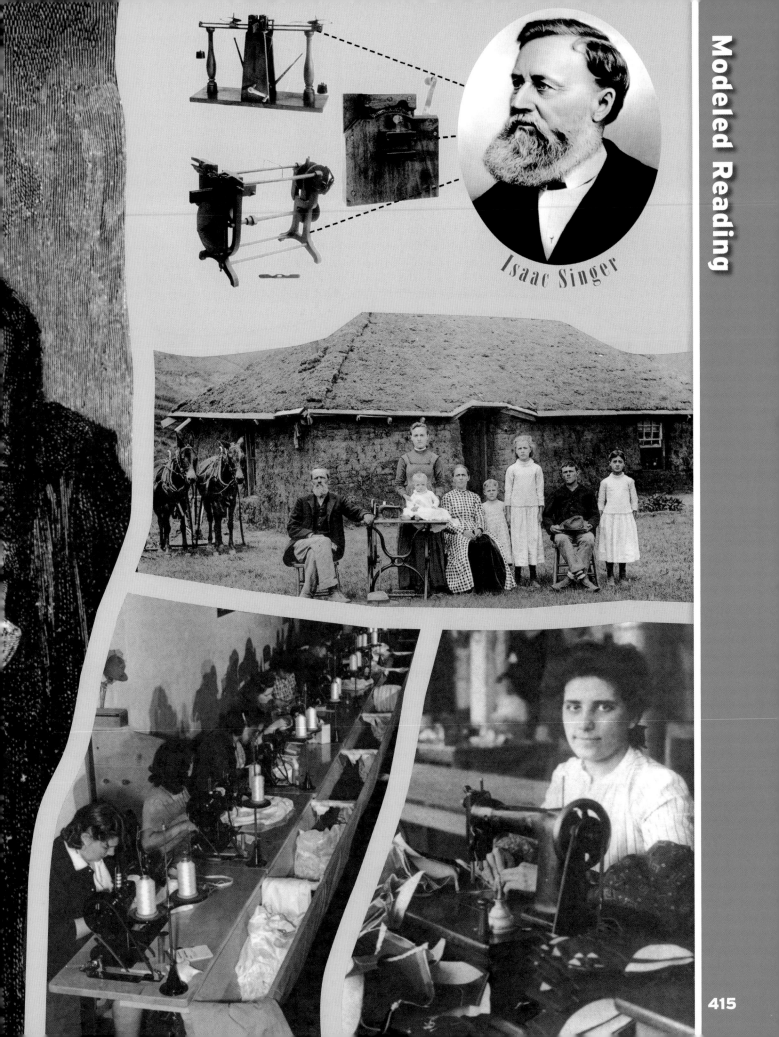

Isaac Singer

STICK IT TO ME

A WALK IN THE WOODS

Sometimes even a simple walk in the woods can lead to a great **invention**. That is what happened to George de Mestral. Back in the 1940s, de Mestral returned home from walking his dog only to discover they were both covered in burs. When de Mestral looked at the burs under a microscope, he saw tiny hooks. The burs gave him an idea. The hooks on the burs stuck to the fuzzy material of his pants. Why not make a new type of fastener to replace the zipper? One side of the fastener could have hooks like a bur, and the other side could have fuzzy loops. He decided to **risk** his time and money in acting on his idea.

Burs inspired Velcro.®

HOOKED ON VELCRO®

An idea is one thing. Getting a **patent** is another problem. Creating a functioning product is a third difficulty! Finding the right materials proved difficult. It took many years, but de Mestral finally succeeded. Finally he could **manufacture** his product. De Mestral even chose a **brand** for his product—the name Velcro®! Velcro® is a combination of the French words *velour* (velvet) and *crochet* (hook).

Velcro® Strap

Structured Vocabulary Discussion

When your teacher says a vocabulary word, your small group will take turns saying the first word you think of. After a few seconds, your teacher will say "Stop." The last person in your group who said a word should explain how that word is related to the vocabulary word your teacher started with.

Throughout the week, add to your vocabulary journal entries. Record new insights and other words that relate to this week's vocabulary.

Picture It

Copy this word organizer into your vocabulary journal. Fill in the ovals with words that describe manufacture, and list examples in the boxes of products people **manufacture**.

manufacture

technical

computers

Copy this word web into your vocabulary journal. Fill in the circles with examples of **inventions**.

cotton gin

invention

Synthesize

Create a Summary

One way that you can synthesize information is to create a summary. A summary is a retelling of the important information—or big ideas—in a text. When you create a summary, you do more than simply list the big ideas. You bring the information together into a meaningful description.

A SUMMARY contains the most important ideas from the text.

To create a summary, find the big ideas. Then bring the ideas together into a meaningful, short description.

TURN AND TALK Listen to your teacher read the following lines from *Queen of Inventions*. With a partner, read the lines and talk about the big ideas. Then discuss answers to the following questions.

• What are the big ideas about the kinds of items that needed to be stitched?

• What are the big ideas about the importance of the sewing machine?

Everything that had been made by hand could now be stitched speedily and sturdily with a machine. Machines were used to stitch boots and shoes, as well as suitcases, horse collars, mailbags, grain sacks, corsets, purses, caps, leather gloves, parasols, straw hats, theater curtains, military uniforms, flags, fire hoses, and even hot-air balloons.

TAKE IT WITH YOU To create a summary, you must first determine the big ideas and then bring together the important information into a meaningful description. As you read other selections, use a chart like the one below to help create summaries.

Most Important Details

The sewing machine worked quickly.

Items made using the sewing machine were sturdy.

Stitched items included boots, shoes, suitcases, horse collars, mailbags, grain sacks, corsets, purses, caps, gloves, parasols, hats, curtains, uniforms, flags, fire hoses, and hot-air balloons.

Summary

Many kinds of items made of fabric or leather—not just clothing—had to be stitched. The sewing machine stitched sturdily and did the job much faster than hand stitching. With the sewing machine, many different products could be manufactured faster and at less cost than before.

HANK, MAKE YOUR BED!

by M. J. Cosson

"Hank, did you . . . ?" Mom called upstairs from the kitchen, which doubles as her control center for tracking family members.

"Don't I every single day?" I responded with a hint of resentment.

"Is it as neat as possible?" she asked.

"Just as a cumulus cloud is lovely and puffy, so is my bed," I replied, trying to make her laugh.

Mom knit her eyebrows. "Hmmm. Puffy isn't exactly neat."

That did it. I decided to invent a bed-making machine that would solve my problem and those of kids throughout the world with tidy mothers who find enjoyment in neatness. I'd be rich enough to retire before I even hit labor-force age!

After math class, my teacher and I sketched a plan with all the necessary measurements. When I got home from school, I rummaged through the garage for materials. I found wood and clamps and hinges to make a mechanical arm and the body of the machine. But the heart of my invention was an old fan. It provided the power to move the arm. I spent the next hours measuring, sawing, hammering, taping, and wiring.

Like a champion athlete, I worked until my brain was fried, my fingers were numb, and my eyes were bleary. The next morning, I made my bed for the last time. I was shooting for completion of my invention that very night.

It was hard to pay attention in school, because I was so excited. After school, I ran home and got to work. Soon I was ready to test my invention. I flipped the switch, hoping for success.

As the fan blade slowly revolved, it raised the wooden arm attached to my covers with one effortless motion. Excellent! Then suddenly the wooden arm came down like a wood-chopping hatchet, splintering as it hit the floor. The arm bounced up and nearly shattered my window. As I sat looking at the mess, my mother called, "Henry, are you cleaning your room?"

Well, Mom, it looks like I definitely am.

The Perfect Pet?

Dear Lydia,

I had a great time visiting you. Ever since I got home, I've been driving my parents crazy talking about your dog, Dooley. I told them that Dooley is a great companion. Finally, I decided to ask my parents for a dog. I told them to think about how much happiness a puppy would bring.

Mom and Dad admitted that a dog would bring a lot of enjoyment. But they said no. They reminded me that we live in a high-rise apartment with a "No Pets" policy. My parents could see my disappointment, so they came up with another suggestion—a robot dog! My dad thinks it is a perfect pet—none of the messiness of a real dog. You know my dad; he loves any advancement in technology. He likes the fact that robot dogs pay attention to voice commands. I'll keep you posted on any developments in my quest for a mechanical Dooley.

Love, Maria

Suffixes *-ness*, *-ion*, *-tion*, and *-ment*

Activity One

About Suffixes

A suffix is a word part added to the end of a root word that changes the word's meaning. Examples of suffixes are *-ness*, *-ion*, *-tion*, and *-ment*. If you add *-ment* to the verb *enjoy*, you get the noun *enjoyment*. You may have to change the spelling of the root word when you add a suffix, such as when you add *-ness* to *happy* to form *happiness*. As your teacher reads *The Perfect Pet?* listen for words with the suffixes *-ness*, *-ion*, *-tion*, and *-ment*.

Suffixes in Context

Read *The Perfect Pet?* and make a list of all the words with the suffixes *-ness*, *-ion*, *-tion*, and *-ment*. Create a chart like the one below, and write down each word, its suffix, and the root word. Remember that the spelling of some root words changes when a suffix is added.

WORD	SUFFIX	ROOT
happiness	ness	happy

Activity Two

Explore Words Together

With a partner, think of as many words as you can that can be made into new words by adding the suffixes *-ness*, *-ion*, *-tion*, and *-ment*. Use the words listed at the right to get started.

connect   fuse

careless   astonish

entertain   educate

Activity Three

Explore Words in Writing

Use some of the words you listed in Activities One and Two to write a paragraph describing the advantages and disadvantages of owning a robot dog. Exchange paragraphs with a partner and circle the suffixes in your partner's paragraph.

Bill Gates

by Jeanie Stewart

How many computers does your school have? Do you have one at home? Does your public library have computers? Not so long ago personal computers were only a dream. Now they seem to be everywhere. But computers might not be so popular if it weren't for people like Bill Gates. Gates, like many others, helped improve and simplify computer technology. These amazing advancements have helped make computers an important part of daily life.

> How did Bill Gates help make computers an important part of daily life?

A Smart Boy with a Head for Computers and Business

William Henry Gates III—Bill to his friends—was born in 1955. He is the second of William and Mary Gates' three children. Bill and his sisters grew up in Seattle, Washington. Bill's father was a lawyer. His mother was a teacher. When Bill was 13, his parents enrolled him in Lakeside School. The decision was fateful. The school introduced Bill to computers.

Young Bill Gates

0/010/0/0/0/
0/6/0/0/6/0/0/00
0/0/0/6/6/6/
0/6/0/0/0/0/0/
0/0/0/0/6/6/
0/0/0/0/0/0/0/
0/6/0/0/0/0/
6/0/6/0/6/0/
0/0/6/0/0/0/
0/0/6/0/0/0/
6/0/0/

Lakeside School

In 1968, computers were huge and complicated. They were also very expensive. Thus, most schools could not afford to own a computer. Lakeside School raised a few thousand dollars to buy time on a computer owned by General Electric. General Electric charged the school based on the number of hours students used the computer. The school thought it had raised enough money to last all year. The school was wrong. It hadn't figured on Bill Gates and his friend Paul Allen.

Bill, Paul, and a few other students were so drawn to this computer that they spent every minute they could on it. In fact, they spent so much time on the computer that they got in trouble for ignoring their homework. In just a few months, Bill and the others used up all of the school's computer time. School officials were not happy at their actions.

> How did Bill Gates and his friends react to being able to use the computer?

The IBM 5150 personal computer was introduced in 1981.

The Computer Center Corporation heard about Bill and his friends. The company offered Lakeside School a deal for computer time. The boys immediately began exploring the new machine. Before long, the boys were causing problems, though. They crashed the system several times. Again they ran up huge bills. The company and the school were not pleased with the latest developments. Bill and his friends were banned from using the computer for six weeks.

A Computer Genius

Computer Center Corporation, which Bill called *C-cubed* (C^3), was having troubles. Its computer crashed often. The computer's security was also weak. No one knew this better than Bill and his friends, who had formed the Lakeside Programming Group. Bill and the group agreed to find the bugs in the system. In return, *C-cubed* gave the group as much free computer time as they wanted.

It was not unusual for Bill to spend all night hunting for bugs. Bill worked to learn everything he could about the computer. He read books and talked to the company's employees. He studied the computer itself. Bill would eventually put the things he learned to use when he helped found Microsoft.

How did Bill learn more about programming?

Computer
Center
x Corporation
C^3!

Young Bill learning about computers

A Young Businessman

By the time *C-cubed* went out of business, Bill and the school group were ready to put their computer skills to use in other places. Another company hired the group to design a payroll program. Once again the group members were given free computer time. And for the first time, the boys actually got paid. The school group was now a real business.

Another of the group's projects was Traf-O-Data. The product was a computer system designed for traffic flow measurement. Lakeside also sought the boys' help. The school hired the group to create a scheduling system. Then, when Bill was a senior, the defense company TRW heard about his talents. The company had a bug-infested computer similar to the one at *C-cubed*. TRW asked Bill and the group to find the bugs and to fix them.

C^3
Traf-O-Data

TRW

> How did the Lakeside Programming Group put their computer skills to work?

Bill Gates (lower left), Paul Allen (lower right), and Microsoft co-workers. December, 1978.

After Lakeside School

At 17, Bill headed off to college, but he never stopped looking for business deals. In 1975, when Bill was 19, he and Paul Allen formed Microsoft. The team launched their software company at the right time. Personal computers were just coming on the market. They all needed software to run.

Bill Gates believes success requires hard work. He says that if you are smart and know how to apply what you know, you can accomplish anything. This belief was certainly true for Bill Gates. Microsoft's success has grown along with computer sales. Today, Microsoft is the largest computer software company in the world.

Microsoft founders Paul Allen and Bill Gates

What do you think the line graph says about the effect of computers on daily life?

mi'cro soft

micro soft

m'icrosoft

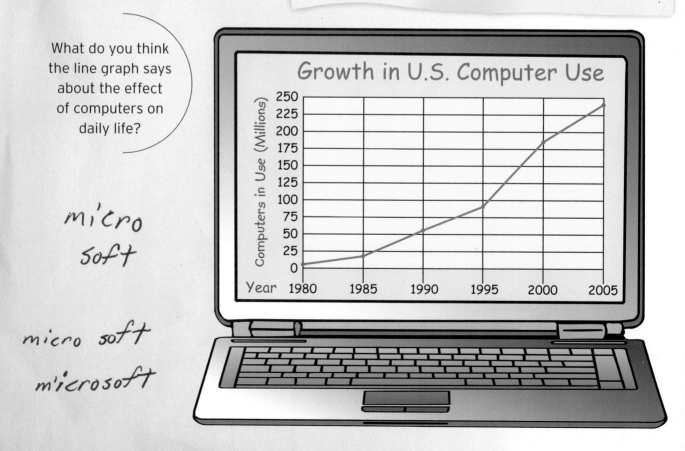

Growth in U.S. Computer Use

Computers in Use (Millions)

Year: 1980, 1985, 1990, 1995, 2000, 2005

Think and Respond

Reflect and Write

- You and your partner have retold the big ideas of each section of *Bill Gates*. Discuss these responses.

- Work with your partner to create a summary of the selection. Choose one big idea for every page. Write down each big idea on an index card. Then put the big ideas together for your summary.

Suffixes in Context

Reread *Bill Gates* to find examples of words with the suffixes *-ness*, *-ion*, *-tion*, and *-ment*. Then work with a partner to use the words to create a word web that describes Bill Gates' experiences with computers at Lakeside School. Share your word web with the class.

Turn and Talk

SYNTHESIZE: CREATE A SUMMARY

Discuss with a partner what you have learned so far about creating a summary.

- What is a summary?

- How do you create a summary?

Explain to your partner how you determined the big ideas and how you used them to create the summary.

Critical Thinking

In a group, discuss how Bill Gates became interested in computers and where that interest led him. List the ways in which Bill Gates learned about computers and software and how he put his knowledge to work. Then, discuss answers to these questions.

- Why do you think the author says that it was fateful that Bill Gates enrolled in Lakeside School?

- How do you think Bill Gates' early experience with computers was unusual for the 1960s and 1970s?

- How was Bill Gates' involvement with computers as a teenager similar to or different from the experience of typical students today?

Vocabulary

Cell Phones OF THE FUTURE

The cell phone is one modern **device** that many people say they can't live without. Cell phones make it possible for family and friends to reach you with **ease** from almost anywhere. That can be a real plus for busy people on the go.

Already many of today's cell phones do more than simply make and receive calls. New phones have a variety of **amazing** features to **simplify** what you need to carry. Some phones take pictures. Others download music, receive e-mails, and surf the Internet. Some phones even let you watch television or play games.

But future cell phones will have new features that may really **astonish** you. Engineers are already working on the design for smart phones. Smart phones will study your habits and know whether it is an appropriate time to ring. The smart phone will also be able to talk to other devices, such as your family car. Think about a phone that can tell how fast a car is moving and whether it is convenientto ring. Now that's astonishing!

Structured Vocabulary Discussion

Work with a partner or in a small group to fill in the following blanks. Be sure you can explain how the words are related.

Startle is to *frighten* as _____ is to *surprise*.

Subtract is to *number* as *use* is to _____.

Throughout the week, add to your vocabulary journal entries. Record new insights and other words that relate to this week's vocabulary.

Picture It

Copy this word organizer into your vocabulary journal. Fill in the boxes with examples of things that you can do with **ease**.

ease
ride a bike

Copy this word wheel into your vocabulary journal. Fill in each section of the circle with an example of a **device**.

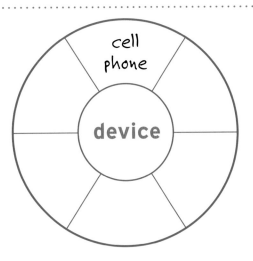

cell phone

device

Lives Spun of Silk

by Abby Jones

"I spin," said Spider.

"I invent," said Human Being.

"Our work has filled our lives with ease."

"My threads help me move and
swing here and there."

"I travel in trains,
planes, and automobiles."

"We can travel great distances."

"I find shelter from weather
in my blanket of silk."

"My home can be heated or cooled
as I wish."

"I capture my meals
in a woven trap."

"I grow food in rows, and
bring it home in sacks."

"We connect with our worlds through the reach of webs."

"I spin to live."

"I live to invent."

*"Though we labor and sweat to make the lives we live
The lives we create are lives spun of silk."*

Go Anywhere MUSIC

Dear Diary,

My vacation at my aunt and uncle's went fairly quickly. I spent my time largely in Uncle Ed's family room. Uncle Ed has nearly 3,000 old vinyl records and new CDs. The music was really great, but it sure took up a lot of room!

Uncle Ed has the recordings carefully lined up on shelves along a long wall. The shelves entirely cover the wall! Uncle Ed's record and CD player and all of his speakers take up a lot of space on another wall. I asked Uncle Ed what he did when he needed to find a record quickly. He smiled cheerfully and said it was hardly ever a problem. Aunt Sally winked. Later Aunt Sally told me that Uncle Ed can't always successfully locate what he wants. I think I'll stick with my MP3 player. All I have to do is slide my music collection in my pocket and I'm ready to go.

Night for now,

Amanda

Suffixes *-ly* and *-fully*

Activity One

About Suffixes

When the suffixes *-ly* and *-fully* are added to the end of a root word, the endings change the word into an adverb, a word that describes a verb, adjective, or other adverb. For example, if you add *-ly* to the adjective *cheap*, you get the adverb *cheaply*. As your teacher reads *Go Anywhere Music*, listen for words with the suffixes *-ly* and *-fully*.

Suffixes in Context

Read *Go Anywhere Music* and list all the words with the suffixes *-ly* and *-fully*. Create a chart like the one below. Write down each word, its suffix, its root word, and the part of speech of the root word.

ADVERB	SUFFIX	ROOT	PART OF SPEECH
quickly	-ly	quick	adjective

Activity Two

Explore Words Together

With a partner, think of as many words as you can that can be made into new words by adding the suffixes *-ly* and *-fully*. Use the words listed at the right to get started.

astounding	dense
blank	grace
hope	vague

Activity Three

Explore Words in Writing

Use some of adverbs you listed in Activities One and Two to write five sentences about the modern inventions you most enjoy. Exchange sentences with a partner and circle the suffixes in your partner's sentences.

Emilia and the Birthday Party

by Elise Oliver

Once upon a time (not long ago at all, really), there was a girl named Emilia. Emilia lived in a big house with her father and stepmother and her two older stepsisters, Anna and Sofia. One Saturday morning, Emilia woke up with a startled jump. Today was the day of Kim's big party! How could she have forgotten? Emilia simply had to be there. Kim was Emilia's best friend. The party was going to be spectacularly great.

Emilia wanted to start getting ready to go right after breakfast. But all of a sudden she groaned and sat down on her bed with a thump. Emilia had put off doing her chores all week. Now she had mountains of laundry and dishes to do, floors to scrub, windows to wash, and her whole room to clean. Her parents had warned Emilia and her stepsisters that chores always had to be done before they could leave the house on weekends. Emilia wouldn't be able to go anywhere until the house was spotless. How could she ever get all of it finished in time for the party?

What is your purpose for reading this text?

Emilia looked at the clock by her bed—9 A.M. Kim's party would start at 2 P.M. That meant that Emilia had five hours to get all of her chores done. Suddenly, Emilia jumped up off her bed and threw on jeans and a tee shirt. If she moved as fast as she could, she just might make it to the party after all!

Three hours later, Emilia was exhausted. Things were simply not going well. Emilia had already broken her dad's favorite coffee mug as she rushed to wash the dishes. She had soap bubbles in her hair, and she had slipped on the water she had spilled in the kitchen. Emilia looked around the room at the towering stacks of laundry and dishes she still had left to do. Her heart sank in despair. Only two hours until the party, and she hadn't even started on the windows or cleaning her bedroom. Emilia wished she could have asked Anna and Sofia to help her, but they were both gone. Her stepsisters had finished their own chores days ago.

Do you think it is important that you understand the meaning of *exhausted*? Explain your answer.

By 1 P.M. Emilia was losing hope. "It's definitely too late now," she said in a quivering voice, "I'll never get this work done and have time to get dressed and ready for the party. I may as well give up."

"Who are you talking to, dear?" said a strange voice. Emilia leapt to her feet and spun around to see an older woman in an old-fashioned, puffy white dress sitting at the kitchen table. "Who are you?" Emilia asked breathlessly.

"Why, I'm your Fairy Godmother, of course."

"Fairy Godmother?" Emilia asked, frowning and more than a little irritated. "Like from a kids' story or something?"

The woman laughed, "Oh, I suppose you don't believe in such things?" The woman smiled, getting up from the table. "Well, Miss Emilia, call it what you like, but the fact is, I'm your Fairy Godmother and I'm here to rescue you at the last minute. That's the way we like to do things, you see—it makes it so dramatic and exciting!"

"You seem so relaxed, like we have all the time in the world," Emilia whined.

"Yes, yes, we'll get this work done. So, how many loads of laundry do you have left to do?"

What information would be important to understand on this page?

438

"Eight," Emilia grumbled. "And I still have one stack of dishes, and the windows and floors, and my room. . . ."

The fairy Godmother broke in, growing impatient, "All right! So, we need a washing machine that can do eight loads of laundry at once, a huge dishwasher, and a Winfloor-Clutter-Buster."

"A what?" Emilia laughed.

"Oh, you'll see. I've invented an absolutely amazing device that will truly astonish you." Fairy Godmother snapped her fingers, and Emilia heard a loud clanging, banging noise coming through the doorway. Suddenly, a huge machine with ten long, swinging metal arms rolled into the kitchen, swiveling and turning this way and that. One long metal arm held a scrub brush that scoured the floor. Another arm picked up the clutter on the counters and put it away. A third arm sprayed the windows. A fourth arm wiped the windows with paper towels.

What strategies could you use to help you figure out the important information on this page?

Emilia just stared. The huge machine rolled over and took stacks of clean dishes out of a giant dishwasher. Turning, Emilia saw an equally large washing machine in the laundry room. "Wow," she breathed.

"Extra-large capacity," Fairy Godmother giggled. "It can do eight loads at once. Go get ready for the party! You must promise me that you'll be home by 6 P.M., in time for dinner."

Emilia smiled gratefully. "I promise. You're the best, Fairy Godmother!"

At 2 P.M. that very afternoon, Emilia was sitting in Kim's dining room surrounded by friends. There were games and cake and prizes. Just as she knew it would be, Kim's party was the best one ever.

Emilia returned home on time. As she walked into the sparkling kitchen, her father and stepmother both ran over to give her a big hug. "The house looks wonderful!" they said proudly.

Emilia sat down at the dinner table, a huge smile on her face. The day had been like a fairy tale. Still, she had learned a lesson. Emilia decided that she'd never put off doing her chores until the last minute ever again.

How can your purpose for reading help you figure out the most important idea in the story?

440

Think and Respond

Reflect and Write

- You and your partner have read *Emilia and the Birthday Party* and explained what you were thinking. Discuss your thoughts.

- On one side of an index card, write an important idea in the story. On the other side, write how your purpose for reading helped you understand the important information.

Suffixes in Context

Reread *Emilia and the Birthday Party* to find examples of the suffixes *-ly* and *-fully*. Write down the words you find. Then use the words to create a description of your own favorite labor-saving device. Exchange descriptions with a partner. Then, circle the suffixes in your partner's description.

Turn and Talk Review

MONITOR UNDERSTANDING: REFLECT ON PURPOSE

Discuss with a partner how reflecting on your purpose helps you.

- What does it mean to reflect on your purpose for reading?

- How does reflecting on your purpose help you decide about important information?

Choose one example of something that was unclear to you while reading *Emilia and the Birthday Party*. Explain to a partner how you decided whether you could read on.

Critical Thinking

With a partner, discuss how the fairy godmother in *Emilia and the Birthday Party* uses inventions to solve Emilia's problem. Write down what Emilia's problems are and list the devices the fairy godmother uses to solve them. Then discuss answers to these questions.

- What comparisons can you draw between the different devices in the story and the role of labor-saving devices in the real world?

- What do you think the author wants you to learn from this story?

Galatea of the Spheres, 1952
Salvador Dalí (1904–1989)

 **THEME 15** Nature's Building Blocks

THEME 16 Body Systems

Viewing

This picture was painted by Salvador Dalí, a Spanish artist of the 20th century. Many of his paintings look more like dreams than real life. In this painting, the artist pictured Galatea, a statue in Roman mythology, who was so admired by her creator that she came to life. Galatea is also the name of one of the moons of Neptune and of an asteroid.

1. What do you see? What does it represent?

2. Why do you think it is possible to tell that Dalí meant the picture to be a human face, not a collection of spheres?

3. How are the spheres in this painting similar to planets in the solar system or cells in the human body?

4. Tell why you agree or disagree with the following statement: The spheres in the painting appear to be moving and standing still at the same time.

In This UNIT

In this unit you will read about the structure and functions of plant and animal cells. You will also learn about the circulatory and other body systems.

Nature's Building Blocks

Contents

Modeled Reading

Shared Reading

Interactive Reading

JUNE 29, 1999

written and illustrated by
DAVID WEISNER

Appreciative Listening

Appreciative listening means listening for parts that are funny or amusing. Listen to the focus questions your teacher will read to you.

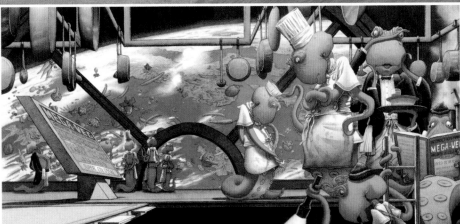

Eggplant Stew for 5,000

Colleyville, Iowa—Last week we were celebrating our good fortune. Five of the giant vegetables that mysteriously fell from space landed in our town. This week we have a big problem of **storage**. Each vegetable is a beautiful **specimen**. But it's a little hard to cram a 1,250-pound onion in the pantry!

Mr. Fernandez, who teaches **biology** at the high school, has explained that the vegetables will soon begin to rot as their cells break down. If we want to **emerge** from this adventure happy, we need to eat. How about eggplant stew for 5,000? Martin's Store has already offered to provide one **element**—the 52 cups of paprika. Tanner's Farm will supply the garlic. Does anyone have a really large stew pot?

- one 1,875-pound eggplant, sliced in bite-size cubes
- one 1,250-pound onion, chopped
- one 625-pound red bell pepper, chopped
- 2,500 garlic cloves, chopped
- 6,250 plum tomatoes, peeled and chopped
- 586 quarts dried chick peas, soaked overnight and drained
- 29 gallons olive oil
- 9 gallons tomato paste
- 52 cups paprika
- 312 cups chopped parsley

In a large stew pot, cook eggplant, onion, bell pepper, and garlic in olive oil until soft. Add remaining ingredients and cook until done. Serve hot or cold.

Structured Vocabulary Discussion

Work with a partner to fill in the following blanks. When you're finished, share your answers with the class. Be sure you can explain your word choices.

Water was the most important _____ in the mixture.

The butterfly will _____ from its cocoon soon.

Throughout the week, add to your vocabulary journal entries. Record new insights and other words that relate to this week's vocabulary.

Picture It

Copy this word web into your vocabulary journal. Fill in the circles with things you can use for **storage**.

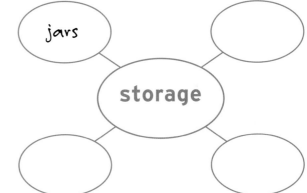

Copy this word organizer into your vocabulary journal. Fill in the ovals with words that mean the same as **specimen**, and list in the boxes examples of things that can be specimens.

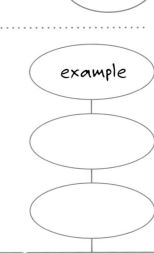

Create Images

Use Visuals

Many selections you read include illustrations, charts, graphs, diagrams, and other visuals. As you read these selections, create a picture in your mind of the information from the visuals. Creating a mental image will help you interpret the information presented in the visual.

VISUALS in the text can help you understand what you read.

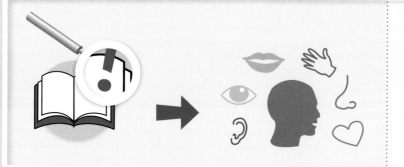

Use visuals to help you create mental images.

TURN AND TALK With a partner look at the illustration on page 447 that shows the Arcturians watching their giant vegetables float through space. Study the information in the illustration. After examining the illustration, listen to your teacher read the lines below from *June 29, 1999.* Then, discuss answers to the following questions with your partner.

- What information do you learn from the illustration?

- How does the information in the illustration help you know something about Holly's experiment that she does not know?

> The place is the ionosphere. On June 29, the Arcturian starcruiser Alula Borealis was touring its sixth planet in four days, and the captain had just pointed out the fjords of Norway off the port side.
>
> In the galley an assistant fry cook accidentally jettisoned the entire food supply. As their vegetables drifted toward the small blue planet below, everyone on board had the same thought: Where would their supper come from?

TAKE IT WITH YOU Try to create mental images of visual features as you read. This will help you interpret important information. Use a chart like the one below to help you remember and apply the information.

Preview the text and place a ✔ next to the visual you find.

☑ **Illustration**   ☑ **Chart**   ☑ **Time Line**
☑ **Photograph**   ☑ **Map**   ☑ **Graph**

Type of visual	How does this visual feature help me to create mental images?
The visual shows the galley of the Arcturian starcruiser. Two Arcturians are looking at a computer terminal.	The visual helps me understand how the vegetables drifted to Earth. It also helps me understand that to the Arcturians, the vegetables are not giants.

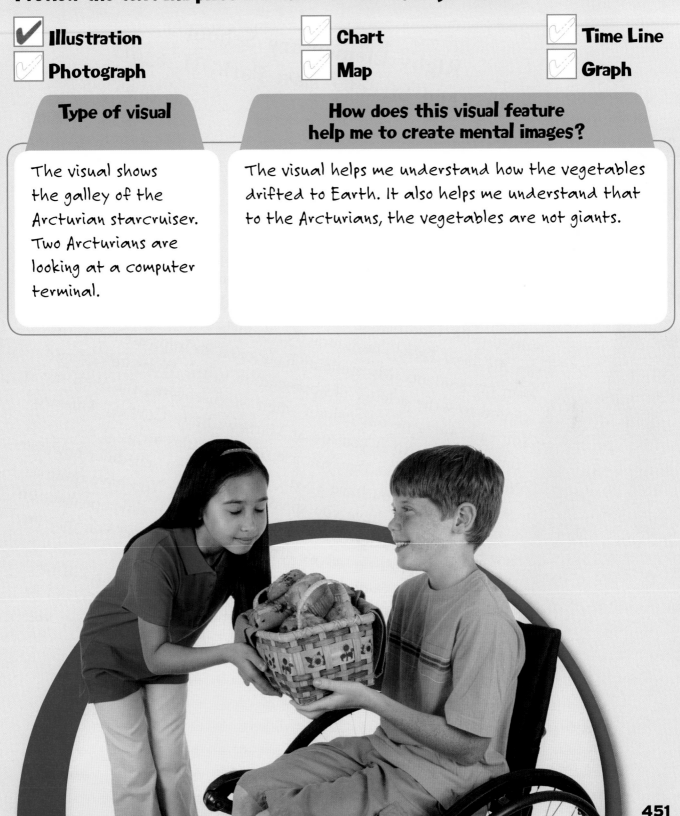

We Would Like to Invite You . . .

Rigby Elementary School
1910 Reed Street • East Park, IL 62017

March 29, 2007

Dr. Miguel Silva
Department of Biology
Mathews State College
137 Central Avenue
Mathews, IL 62049

Dear Dr. Silva:

My fifth grade class has just begun a science unit on plant and animal cells. One of the resources we find most useful is the Web site *All About Cells.* The interactive models always get a "Wow!" from my students. My students have been so impressed that they wanted to write a letter of appreciation to the Web site's creator. You can't imagine our delight when we discovered the Web site is your creation. AND you are at Mathews State College. Amazing! We couldn't believe that you are only 30 miles away.

We are sure you have a very busy teaching schedule; however, we would love to have you speak to the class. You have quite a few fans here at Rigby. We normally try to schedule speakers on Mondays or Fridays, but we are so anxious to meet you that any day would be wonderful.

I have enclosed a map to Rigby in hopes that you will be able to fit us into your schedule. Either call me at 555-2783 or respond via email, please. I look forward to hearing from you.

Sincerely,

Sue Miller
Fifth Grade Teacher

Animalcules

December 5, 1676

Dear Diary,

Amazing! That is the only way to describe my day. I've just come from meeting with Anton van Leeuwenhoek (LAY-wen-hook). I read his paper about viewing living creatures under a microscope, and I had to see them for myself. Unbelievable! I actually saw the tiny creatures move about in water. These creatures where so small that I saw nothing without the microscope!

I have been lucky enough to see Robert Hooke's drawings of cork cells. He drew them after looking at a sliver of cork under a microscope. Each cell looks like a tiny empty chamber, but there are hundreds of cells in a drawing. Hooke thinks that a one-inch square of cork has more than one billion cells. Astounding! The drawings are quite impressive; however, they are nothing compared to seeing something move.

Leeuwenhoek calls his creatures "animalcules" (AN i mah Kyuls). They are so small that a hundred laid end-to-end are no bigger than a grain of coarse sand. He is able to see the creatures because his microscopes are so powerful. Some can enlarge a creature to almost 300 times its size. Imagine that!

Martin

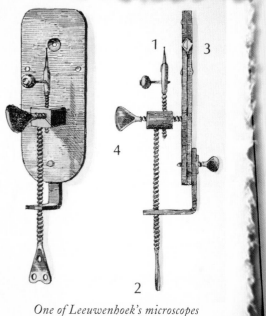

One of Leeuwenhoek's microscopes

Conjunctions and Interjections

Activity One

About Conjunctions and Interjections

A conjunction is a word that connects words, groups of words, or sentences. Some conjunctions join equal parts, such as *and*, *but, or, nor,* and *for.* Some conjunctions come in pairs, such as *either/or* and *both/and.* Some conjunctions, such as *because, however,* and *that,* join two clauses to make a complex sentence. Interjections are words or groups of words that express strong feelings. *Help!* is an example of an interjection. As your teacher reads *Animalcules* listen for conjunctions and interjections.

Conjunctions and interjections in Context

With a partner, read *Animalcules* to find conjunctions and interjections. Write the conjunction or interjection in a chart like the one below. Then, explain the function the word or phrase serves.

CONJUNCTION OR INTERJECTION	FUNCTION
Amazing!	Interjection showing surprise
and	Conjunction joining two sentences

Activity Two

Explore Words Together

Look at the list of conjunctions and interjections on the right. Take turns with a partner providing examples of how the words or phrases can be used.

Wow!   although
either   Of course!
Oops!   if

Activity Three

Explore Words in Writing

Think about things you have looked at or would like to look at under a microscope. Write three sentences describing the experience. Use conjunctions and interjections in your sentences. Share your sentences with a partner.

INSIDE JOB

by Kathleen Powell

"Five minutes and counting," a voice warned over the sub's radio. "Alert!"

Ali couldn't contain her excitement. Several years before, her father had developed a method of shrinking a submarine smaller than a cell. Using the sub, he could enter a fruit cell and change its DNA. His company now produced the world's tastiest fruit! Today her father was going to change DNA to produce a larger, sweeter orange, and Ali was going along!

Ali waited in the submarine for the adventure to begin. Bursting with questions, she asked, "Dad, how will we alter the DNA?"

"Not now, honey," her dad answered quickly. He was reviewing a checklist and looking very serious.

Ali knew that DNA is the material in a cell that determines the features of a living thing. Ali had dark hair and dark eyes thanks to DNA.

"Ten seconds and counting," the voice on the radio cautioned.

Ali's father smiled at her, "Get ready!"

How might the illustration on this page give you an idea of what the story is about before you start reading?

"Three . . . two . . . one . . . ," the voice on the radio continued the coutdown.

"Ouch!" Ali said as she felt a tingly sensation run through her body. Outside the submarine's window, the room seemed to grow bigger and bigger. Then, suddenly, the shrinking stopped, but they weren't small enough to fit in a cell. "Is something wrong, Dad?" Ali inquired nervously.

What mental images of the shrinking process does the illustration on this page help you form?

Her father laughed reassuringly. "No, Ali, this is just the first shrink stage—look outside the submarine."

"Oh!" Ali gasped as she watched a giant hand outside the window lift the submarine and move it toward the petri dish on what was now a huge table.

"We shrink in two stages," her dad explained. "First, the beams make us small enough to fit in a petri dish. The petri dish contains a special gel that scientists have placed orange cells inside. Once we're in the gel, the beams will make us much smaller so that we can move into the cell and transform the DNA. Until recently, scientists transformed DNA without the help of submarines, but subs are more reliable, and they do the job faster."

Two-Word Technique
Write down two words that reflect your thoughts about each page. Discuss them with your partner.

Ali felt the tingly sensation again. Everything became shades of gray. The room outside looked blurry.

"OK," her dad explained, "we've shrunk to the necessary size. Now, let's find that orange cell." Her father started the engine, and the submarine sped through the gel. Ali could see cells that looked the size of buildings passing swiftly by the submarine's window.

Her father was busy pushing buttons and checking dials; however, he stopped every so often to describe what was happening. "Sensors will identify the orange cell." After a few minutes, Ali heard a beeping sound.

"Has it found the cell?" Ali asked excitedly.

"Yes. Hold on!" her father instructed.

The orange cell looked like an enormous building surrounded by cushions. Ali's father aimed toward the side. Ali cried "Whoa!" as the submarine struggled to enter.

Moments later, her father announced, "We've moved through the cell wall, and we're now going through the cell membrane."

How do the illustrations on this page match what you know about cells or submarines? Explain.

Once through the membrane, the ride was smoother. Ali and her father entered a huge area with lots of floating objects. It was beautiful!

"What are those things?" Ali asked, astounded.

Her dad smiled at Ali's wonder. "We're inside the cell now. The various objects have different jobs to keep the cell running, like workers in a factory."

He pointed toward something that looked like a giant balloon filled with dark shapes. That's the vacuole—it's the cell's storage area."

Ali hadn't realized a cell had so many parts. "Where's the DNA?" she asked, peering around at all of the different objects.

"The DNA is in the nucleus. Scientists call the nucleus the "brain of the cell" because it controls everything. There is it!" he exclaimed, pointing to a dark ball just ahead. Her father aimed the submarine toward the nucleus. Ali held on tightly as the submarine entered the nucleus. She felt a lurch, and a minute later they were inside. The environment was more complicated here. Ali felt like she had jumped into a bowl of spaghetti!

"Wow! Is that squiggly material DNA?" she asked, laughing.

"Yes, it is," Ali's father replied, smiling.

How could your mental images from this story help you remember facts about the structure of cells?

Ali's dad went right to work. He studied charts and turned on sensors. Then he pushed a button, and giant cutters came out of the submarine. Ali also saw what looked like giant pliers emerge. For the next hour, the submarine moved from one part of the DNA to another, cutting pieces in one place and attaching them in another. Finally, Ali's dad announced, "OK, that's the last—it's time to leave!"

The submarine made its way back through the nucleus, membrane, and cell wall to the surface of the petri dish. Ali's dad informed the workers that the project was complete. Soon, Ali felt the familiar tingle, and she realized they were getting bigger.

The shrinking beams worked in reverse to return the sub to normal size. Smiling workers greeted Ali and her dad. Everyone looked forward to the larger, sweeter oranges that would form. Ali, however, could only think about her amazing voyage inside the cell.

How might your mental image from this story add to your understanding of DNA?

Think and Respond

Reflect and Write

- You and your partner have taken turns reading sections of *Inside Job* and sharing words that reflect your thoughts. Discuss the words you shared and how they related to the text.

- Choose two illustrations from the story. Describe each on an index card. On the other side of each index card, explain how the visual helped you understand the story better.

Conjunctions and Interjections in Context

Reread *Inside Job* to find examples of conjunctions and interjections. Write down the examples you find. Describe one of the illustrations from the story. Use at least three of the conjunctions and two of the interjections in your description. Share your description with a partner.

Turn and Talk

CREATE IMAGES: USE VISUALS

Discuss with a partner what you have learned so far about using visuals.

- What does it mean to use visuals?

- How does creating mental images from visuals help you understand what you read?

Choose one of the mental images you created from visuals while reading *Inside Job*. Explain to a partner how that image helped you interpret the text and illustrations in the story.

Critical Thinking

In a group, discuss what you know about science fiction stories. Write your ideas down on a sheet of paper. Look back at *Inside Job*. Brainstorm with your group a list of the processes Ali and her father went through to accomplish their mission. Write them down on a piece of paper. Then discuss these questions together.

- Why did Ali and her father have to enter the nucleus of the orange cell?

- What steps did Ali's father take to transform the DNA?

- What parts of this science fiction story are true and what parts are fiction?

INSIDE AN ELM

Congratulations on your purchase of an elm tree! To keep your elm tree healthy, keep in mind one **detail**. The beautiful elm can fall victim to Dutch elm disease. Once infected, the tree often dies quickly. Understanding your elm tree's biology will help you understand how the disease spreads.

Tree Infected with Dutch Elm Disease

PLANT BIOLOGY 101 The basic building block of your tree is the **cell**. A tree grows through cell **division**. In cell division, the **nucleus** and its surrounding material split to form new cells. The nucleus is the cell's control center. It contains DNA. DNA is the material that determines the characteristics of a cell. Like most plants, your elm tree has different types of cells. Some cells cover the outer surface of the tree. Some cells form the tree's body. Still others form the tree's circulatory system.

HOW THE DISEASE SPREADS
The tree's circulatory system carries life-giving food and water. However, it can also spread Dutch elm disease. Thus, **arrange** to cut off infected branches immediately. If you wait, it will be too late. Good luck. Enjoy your tree.

Elm Tree

Structured Vocabulary Discussion

When your teacher says a vocabulary word, you and your partner should each write on a piece of paper the first words that come to mind. When your teacher says, "Stop," exchange papers with your partner and explain the words on your lists to each other.

Throughout the week, add to your vocabulary journal entries. Record new insights and other words that relate to this week's vocabulary.

Picture It

Copy this word wheel into your vocabulary journal. In the upper sections, name things you can **arrange**. In the bottom section, name things you cannot arrange.

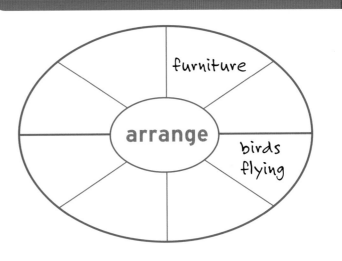

furniture

arrange

birds flying

Copy this word organizer into your vocabulary journal. Fill in the boxes with things you know about **division**.

division

I use division when I cut my sandwich in half.

Diseased Branch

463

Five spring Flowers

Five spring flowers, arranged all in a row.

The first one said, "We need rain to grow!"

The second one said, "Oh, my, we need water!"

The third one said, "Yes, it is getting hotter!"

The fourth one said, "I see clouds in the sky."

The fifth one said, "I wonder why?"

Then BOOM! went the thunder

And ZAP! went the lightning!

That springtime storm was really frightening!

But the flowers weren't worried—no, no, no, NO!

The rain helped them to grow, grow, GROW!

Word Study

Cells
NATURE'S BUILDING BLOCKS

Something to CELL-a-brate! The largest human cell is about the width of a human hair. However, most human cells are much smaller. In fact, it would take somewhere in the neighborhood of 10,000 human cells to cover the head of a pin. With that number as a benchmark, you probably wouldn't be surprised to learn that the average human body has more than 10 trillion cells. That's a lot of cells!

Human cell

What's Your DNA? Cells are the basic building blocks of plant and animal life. Plant and animal cells are similar in many ways. In both types of cells, a cell membrane encloses the cell's nucleus and other structures. The nucleus contains DNA, the cell's genetic blueprint. A jelly-like substance called cytoplasm surrounds the nucleus and other structures. However, plant cells have one clear-cut difference. Unlike animal cells, plant cells have a somewhat rigid outer cell wall. This wall gives the plant cell its shape.

Animal cell

Compound Words

Activity One

About Compound Words

A compound word consists of two or more words used as a single word. Compound words can be closed, open, or hyphenated. As your teacher reads *Cells: Nature's Building Blocks*, listen for compound words.

Plant cell

Compound Words in Context

With a partner, reread *Cells: Nature's Building Blocks*. Write each compound word in a chart like the one below. Then, identify the type of compound word, list the individual words that form it, and provide a definition for the compound word.

COMPOUND WORD	TYPE OF COMPOUND	WORDS IN COMPOUND	DEFINITION OF COMPOUND WORD
somewhere	closed	some where	a place not known

Activity Two

Explore Words Together

With a partner, look at the list of compound words on the right. Discuss what words form each compound. Then, take turns defining the compound words.

openminded	check up
help desk	self-service
doorway	nickname

Activity Three

Explore Words in Writing

Write four sentences that describe how cells are nature's building blocks. Use one compound word in each sentence. Share your favorite sentence with a partner.

Amazing Bamboo

by Nicole Zern

Our science assignment is to create an observation log for something in nature. I have chosen bamboo as the subject of my observation log. Bamboo is an amazing plant. Although it looks like a shrub or a tree, bamboo is actually a member of the grass family. There are more than 1,000 different types of bamboo. Some types grow to less than a foot tall. Other types can grow to over 100 feet tall. The taller varieties are what you see in pictures of bamboo forests.

Bamboo is a very useful plant. People use bamboo as food and building material and even make fabric and paper from its fibers. But the detail I find most amazing is how fast it grows. Bamboo does not grow like a tree. An individual tree gets taller and its trunk gets bigger around each year. An individual bamboo stem— or cane— grows to its full height and weight in about five or eight weeks. This is true even for the tallest canes.

Most bamboo likes warm weather all year round. However, some types can survive colder weather. My observation log will follow the growth of Moso bamboo. It is a giant bamboo that can grow in my area of Alabama.

Moso Bamboo

How could you summarize the information about bamboo on this page?

Preparation

I made my observations on my Aunt Molly's property. Her bamboo forest covers about three acres of land. Moso bamboo spreads by underground stems called "runners." These stems send up new shoots each year. Thus, the forest slowly gets larger as new plants grow from the runners. My aunt has also increased the size of her forest through plant division. Each year she divides one or two bamboo plants into several pieces and plants the pieces in new areas.

The bamboo forest I observed is about six years old. This fact is important because bamboo plants do not begin to grow quickly until the forest is about three years old. After that, each year's canes are larger than those that sprouted the year before. An individual cane grows only the first year. This means that the newest canes are always the tallest.

What details on this page would be important for a summary about bamboo growth?

Bamboo Forest

Bamboo Runner (cross section)

My aunt suggested that I follow the growth of two shoots, in case one shoot died. Before beginning my observations, I created a 30-foot measuring pole, marked off in feet and inches. I placed the pole between two shoots.

April 2, 3:30 P.M.

Bamboo Shoot 1: 5 inches tall

Bamboo Shoot 2: 6 inches tall

Observation: Both shoots are well-defined and look healthy. Shoot 1 is the shortest at 5 inches. It is also the most narrow at the base, measuring only 4.7 inches across. Shoot 2 is 6 inches tall and 5 inches wide. Aunt Molly says that bamboo shoots start out at the width they will be when fully grown—the canes don't get bigger around as they get taller. According to my research, the widest shoot should produce the tallest cane. Thus, I think Shoot 2 will grow to be the taller one of the two shoots.

Read, Cover, Remember, Retell Technique
With a partner, take turns reading as much text as you can cover with your hand. Then cover up what you read and retell the information to your partner.

April 6, 4:15 P.M.

Bamboo Shoot 1: 13 inches (1 foot 1 inch) tall

Bamboo Shoot 2: 15 inches (1 foot 3 inches) tall

Observation: Shoot 1 appears to be growing at a slower rate. Shoot 2 has averaged a little over 2 inches a day; Shoot 1 has averaged just 2 inches. Aunt Molly says the difference in the rate of growth might change over time, but she thinks I am right about which plant will end up being the taller one.

How could you summarize the differences on this page in the observations of the two shoots of bamboo?

April 9, 2:10 P.M.

Bamboo Shoot 1: 25 inches
                 (2 feet 1 inch) tall

Bamboo Shoot 2: 30 inches
                 (2 feet 6 inch) tall

   Observation: Shoot 1 is still growing at a slower rate than Shoot 2. Shoot 1 averages 4 inches a day. Shoot 2 averages 5 inches a day. Aunt Molly says that daily growth will increase dramatically once the canes reach 3 feet.

April 12, 4:30 P.M.

Bamboo Shoot 1: 40 inches (3 feet 4 inches) tall

Bamboo Shoot 2: 50 inches (4 feet 2 inches) tall

   Observation: Shoot 1 has grown at a slightly faster rate than Shoot 2 over the past few days. But it is still the shorter one. I've learned from research that bamboo sometimes grows as much as 3 feet a day. My aunt says that the bamboo usually grows between 1 and 2 feet in Alabama. She says that soil, sunlight, temperature, and rainfall affect growth.

April 13, 4:30 P.M.

Bamboo Shoot 1: 63 inches (5 feet 3 inches) tall

Bamboo Shoot 2: 73 inches (6 feet 1 inch) tall

   Observation: Both shoots have shown a two-foot growth since yesterday! It is not the 3 feet I had hoped for, but it is pretty impressive.

> How could you summarize what happened to the bamboo shoots between April 9 and April 13?

April 15, 4:45 P.M.

Bamboo Shoot 1: 112 inches (9 feet 4 inch) tall

Bamboo Shoot 2: 120 inches (10 feet) tall

Observation: Both shoots continue to grow at just under 2 feet a day. It appears my prediction was well-founded. Shoot 1 will probably not catch up with Shoot 2.

April 20, 4:45 P.M.

Bamboo Shoot 1: 229 inches (19 feet 1 inch) tall

Bamboo Shoot 2: 268 inches (22 feet 4 inches) tall

Observation: Shoot 2 has topped 22 feet in less than 20 days. Both shoots have about 40 more days to grow during the season. At this rate, Shoot 2 should reach 50 feet tall by the end of the growing season.

The following line graph compares the growth of Shoots 1 and 2. The graph shows the height measurements for each of my seven observations. I believe the graph supports the idea that the width and height of a cane are related.

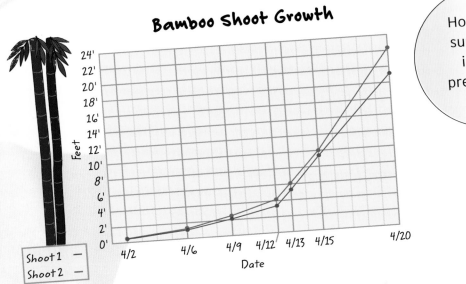

Bamboo Shoot Growth

Shoot 1 —
Shoot 2 —

How would you summarize the information presented in the line graph?

472

Think and Respond

Reflect and Write

- You and your partner took turns reading aloud and retelling sections of *Amazing Bamboo*. Discuss your retellings with your partner.

- Choose two sections in the text and create a summary of each one. Write the big ideas of the section on one side of an index card. Write the summary on the other side of the index card.

Compound Words in Context

Reread *Amazing Bamboo* to find examples of compound words. Then work with a partner to create a poem that uses compound words to describe the growth rate of bamboo. Share your poem with the class.

Turn and Talk

SYNTHESIZE: CREATE A SUMMARY

Discuss with a partner what you have learned so far about how to create a summary.

- How do you synthesize material to create a summary?

Review with a partner the summary you created for *Amazing Bamboo*. Explain to your partner how you used the important ideas to create the summary.

Critical Thinking

In a group, brainstorm a description of how a tree grows. Return to *Amazing Bamboo*, and discuss what you read about how bamboo grows. Then discuss answers to these questions.

- What are the main differences in the way bamboo and a tree grow?

- What factors did Nicole have to consider when setting up her observation?

- What conclusions can you draw from Nicole's observation log?

Contents

Modeled Reading

Shared Reading

Interactive Reading

THE HEART
OUR CIRCULATORY SYSTEM

SEYMOUR SIMON

Strategic Listening

Strategic listening means listening to make sure you understand the selection. Listen to the focus questions your teacher will read to you.

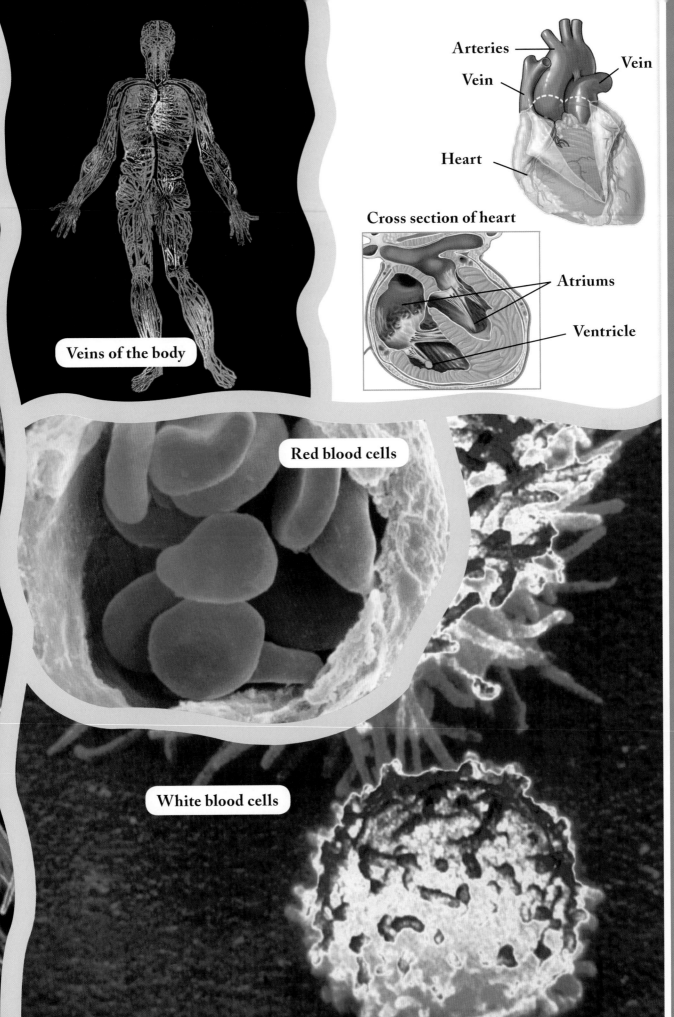

Arteries

Vein

Vein

Heart

Cross section of heart

Atriums

Ventricle

Veins of the body

Red blood cells

White blood cells

BETTER Than the ORIGINAL?

Your heart is a powerful **muscle**. Your heart is so strong that it can pump your total blood supply around your body in about a minute. That's pretty amazing for something that's only about the size of your closed fist. When you are at rest, your heart beats about 70 times a minute.

Heart

Your heart pumps blood by contracting. In a healthy heart, the contractions are strong and regular. However, some people's hearts beat in an **irregular** pattern. Some people have damaged hearts. Their hearts are too weak to pump blood effectively. If the **situation** is serious enough, people need their hearts repaired, or even replaced.

Mechanical Heart

Doctors use two types of artificial hearts to help people with serious heart problems. The most common type is used when doctors are doing surgery on a patient's heart or **lung**. The device is called the heart-lung machine. By temporarily taking over the tasks of the heart and lungs, this machine gives doctors a change to operate. The second type—the mechanical heart—is placed inside the body to replace a failing heart. Mechanical hearts are still experimental. However, many scientists are hopeful. The human body views a transplanted human heart as a foreign **substance**. It tries to reject it. A mechanical heart would solve this problem.

Structured Vocabulary Discussion

When your teacher says a vocabulary word, take turns in a small group saying the first word that comes to mind. When your teacher says, "Stop," the last person in your group who said a word should explain how that word is related to the vocabulary

Throughout the week, add to your vocabulary journal entries. Record new insights and other words that relate to this week's vocabulary.

Picture It

Copy this word organizer into your vocabulary journal. Fill in the boxes with statements about the **lung**.

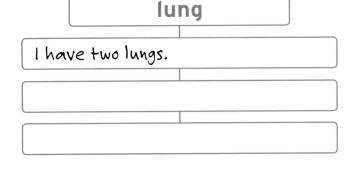

lung

I have two lungs.

Copy this word web into your vocabulary journal. Fill in the circles with things that can be a **substance**.

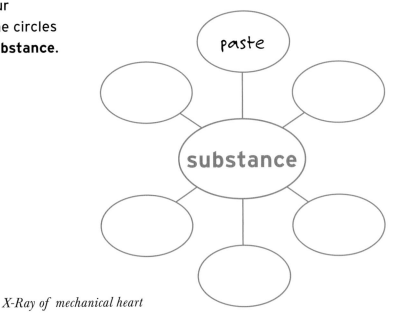

paste

substance

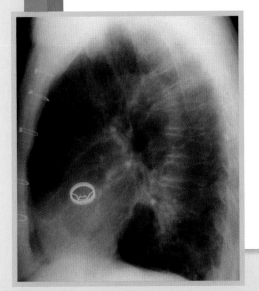

X-Ray of mechanical heart

Use Fix-Up Strategies
Read On

When you run into an idea or word you do not understand, one effective strategy is to read on. The text may have additional information that will explain the unfamiliar word or confusing idea.

When you READ ON, you skip a difficult word and read past it.

When you come to a word or idea you do not understand, read on and use the text that follows to help you figure out the meaning.

TURN AND TALK Listen as your teacher reads the following lines from *The Heart.* Then with a partner, reread the lines and discuss answers to the following questions.

• What words or ideas, if any, caused you problems while you were reading?

• How could you use the strategy of reading on to fix these problems?

Your heart, blood vessels, and blood work together to supply each of your cells with all of its needs. Every minute, the heart pushes a pulsing stream of blood through a network of blood vessels to every cell in your body. The constantly moving blood brings food and oxygen to each cell, carries away such wastes as carbon dioxide, and serves as an important component in the body's immune system. The heart, blood, and web of blood vessels make up your circulatory system.

TAKE IT WITH YOU Reading on when you get stuck on a word will help you understand what you read. As you read other selections, determine the problems you face and decide whether you can fix the problem by reading on. Use a chart like the one below to help you with the process.

Word I Got Stuck On	What I Did				Which One Worked?
	Used Illustrations	Used Phonics	Read On	Broke It into Parts	
component	✓	✓	✓	✓	The text and one illustration provided much more information about the role of blood. Reading on did help me figure out that component might mean "a part."

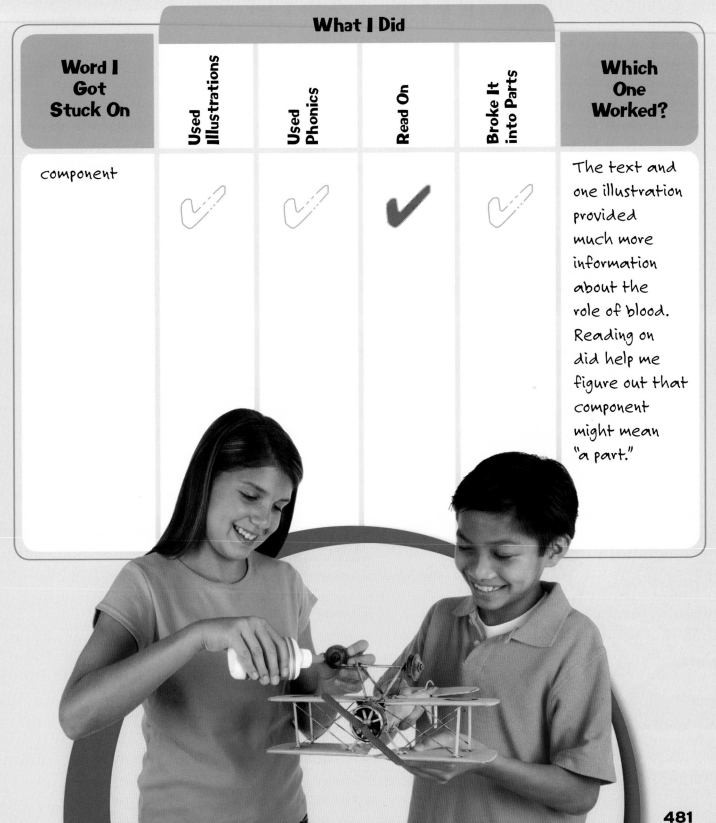

THE TALE OF ACHILLES
A GREEK MYTH

retold by Chris Parker

The ancient Greeks felt that pride was a dangerous emotion. They told many myths in which a great hero becomes too proud. In these myths, the arrogant hero is always punished somehow.

Once, in the lands of ancient Greece, there was a mortal man named Peleus (PEEL-e-us). He married Thetis (THEE-tus), a beautiful nymph, or sea-spirit. They had a son, Achilles (ah-KILL-ees). While he was still an infant, Thetis decided to try to make her son immortal. She did this by dipping the baby in the River Styx, the river of the Underworld. Wherever the wondrous waters touched Achilles, no weapon would be able to harm him. However, as she dipped him in the river, she held him by one heel. That heel did not get wet. As a result, he had one heel that remained mortal and vulnerable.

As Achilles grew up, he learned the skills of running, hunting, and fighting. He became a powerful warrior. When war broke out between the Greeks and the Trojans, Achilles joined the Greek army. Although the Greeks had many great heroes, Achilles was the greatest soldier of them all. He could not be defeated in battle. Of course, no one knew that his heel was his weak spot.

Achilles was also a proud and stubborn man. As the war went on, he offended many of the gods with his arrogant deeds. Then one day, as the fighting raged, a Trojan prince shot an arrow at Achilles. The god Apollo guided the arrow. The arrow flew through the air, hitting Achilles in his heel. The mighty hero died.

Today, we are reminded of the story of Achilles by not one, but two terms in the English language. An "Achilles heel" is a metaphor for a weak point that leads to a person's downfall. The scientific name of the tendon that connects the muscles of the lower leg with the heel bone is the "Achilles tendon."

Smart Food, Smart Choices, Healthy You!

by Alice Leonhardt

It's dinner and you gobble down a big cheeseburger, fries, and a 12-ounce soda. You wolf down a slice of pie before heading to soccer practice. As you are jogging onto the field, your teammate kicks you a ball, but you can barely lift your foot to kick it back. Your legs feel like lead. Your soda, burger, fries, and pie churn in your stomach.

How could you use the read on fix-up strategy to help you understand what is meant by smart foods?

Suddenly, your dinner doesn't seem so yummy. You're too tired to play even though you love soccer (or biking, hiking, skateboarding, or . . . you fill in the fun activity). But you were hungry, and you needed to eat. So why don't you have the energy to play?

You lack energy because what you eat has an immediate impact on how you feel, how quickly you react, and how clearly you think. If you want to do well in sports and school, smart foods are a much better choice than burgers, fries, pie, and soda. Choosing smart foods from the basic food groups listed in the Food Guide Pyramid will help your body defend itself against illness and injury. It will also improve your soccer game. Smart food + smart choices = a healthy, active you.

Your food choices do make a difference. Your body needs protein, vitamins, minerals, and carbohydrates to grow and stay healthy. The soda, burgers, fries, and pie you ate have nutrients. But these foods are also high in fat and sugar. Smart foods not only contain the needed nutrients, they are also low in fat and sugar. Thus, they are the right choice for a healthy lifestyle.

How could you help your understanding if you did not know the meaning of the word *nutrients*?

Protein builds your muscles, organs, and immune system. Meats, poultry, fish, eggs, nuts, seeds, and beans are good sources of protein. However, some protein choices are smarter than others because of the amount and type of fat they contain. Getting a little bit of fat in your diet is healthy—vitamins A, D, E, and K hang around in fat, and these vitamins are important to your body. Fat also helps your brain and heart. However, some fats are healthier than others.

Food Guide Pyramid

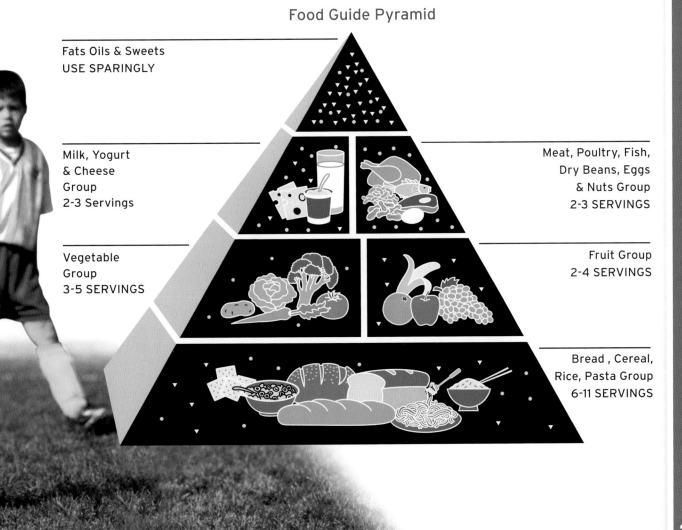

Fats Oils & Sweets
USE SPARINGLY

Milk, Yogurt & Cheese Group
2-3 Servings

Meat, Poultry, Fish, Dry Beans, Eggs & Nuts Group
2-3 SERVINGS

Vegetable Group
3-5 SERVINGS

Fruit Group
2-4 SERVINGS

Bread , Cereal, Rice, Pasta Group
6-11 SERVINGS

Two-Word Technique
Write down two words that reflect your thoughts about each page. Discuss them with your partner.

There are three types of fat: unsaturated, saturated, and trans fat. Unsaturated fat is sometimes called "heart healthy" fat. It's found in olive oil, peanut oil, canola oil, and fish such as salmon and tuna. Eating foods with unsaturated fat is a smart choice. Saturated fats are found in meat, poultry, and dairy products. Eating too much saturated fat is not good for you. Eating lean meats and low-fat dairy products limits the amount of saturated fat you take in. Trans fats are the worst for you and should be limited. Trans fats are found in fried foods, snack foods, and baked goods. Many food companies and restaurants are cutting down on trans fats in their products.

What fix-up strategy could you use to help you understand the difference between trans, saturated, and unsaturated fats? Explain.

Your body also needs vitamins. However, your body can't make vitamins. It gets vitamins from the food you eat. Vitamin A gives you healthy skin and eyes and helps you resist infections. Smart choices for vitamin A include eggs, milk, sweet potatoes, and spinach. The different B vitamins are important for energy. B vitamins also help make red blood cells, which carry oxygen through your body. Smart choices include shrimp, salad greens, yogurt, peas, and wheat bread.

Food Guides Through Time

1894

The U.S. government publishes its first dietary recommendations. Vitamins and minerals have not yet been discovered.

1916

The first food guide–"Food for Young Children"–is published. It contains five food groups: (1) milk and meat, (2) cereal, (3) vegetables and fruits, (4) fats and fatty foods, and (5) sugars and sugary foods.

1943

The Basic Seven food groups are recommended. This becomes the Basic Four: (1) dairy, (2) meats and poultry, (3) fruits and vegetables, and (4) grain products.

Vitamin C keeps your gums and muscles in shape, helps wounds heal, and helps you resist colds. Smart choices include strawberries, orange juice, tomatoes, and broccoli. Vitamin D is necessary for strong bones and teeth. It also helps your body absorb an important mineral called calcium. Smart choices include egg salad, milk, yogurt, and fish. Vitamin E works to protect and maintain your lungs, eyes, skin, and liver and helps form red blood cells. Smart choices include whole wheat bread and crackers, spinach, salad greens, eggs, almonds, and peanuts. Vitamin K helps your blood clot if you get cut. Smart choices include pork, milk, cottage cheese, kale, and leafy lettuce.

Your body also needs minerals to stay healthy. Iron, calcium, magnesium, selenium, and zinc are necessary for producing bones and blood cells. They also help protect cells and fight diseases. You need to eat a variety of foods to get all these minerals. Smart choices include milk, yogurt, tofu, cheese, lean meats, eggs, and raisins.

What could you do if you did not understand the importance of calcium in the body?

1970
A fifth group—fats and sweets, meant to be eaten in moderation—is added to the Basic Four.

1992
The Food Guide Pyramid is created.

2005
"My Pyramid, Steps to a Healthier You" Web site is created.

You also need carbohydrates for energy. There are two types of carbohydrates: simple sugars and complex starches. You need both for a healthy diet. However, not all carbohydrates are smart choices. Some contain only empty calories. Calories are units of energy. Your body burns calories every day. You need calories for running and swimming. You also need them to keep your heart beating and your lungs breathing. Junk foods like candy bars and chips are high in carbohydrates. In these foods, the calories don't come with any useful vitamins and minerals. That's why we say their calories are empty. Grapes, on the other hand, are a great source of vitamins and minerals. They also contain fiber, which helps you digest your food. Other smart choices for carbohydrates include apples, oatmeal, pasta, and berries.

Has reading to the end of the essay cleared up any words or ideas you did not understand at first? Explain your answer.

As you can see, protein, vitamins, minerals, and carbohydrates are all important for your body. If you eat foods loaded with fat and empty calories, your body will know it. So will your soccer game! Instead, choose to eat foods packed with the nutrients needed to fuel your body. Always remember: smart food + smart choices = a healthy, active you!

Think and Respond

Reflect and Write

- You and your partner have read *Smart Food, Smart Choices, Healthy You!* and written two words for each page. Discuss your words and thoughts.

- Choose three words or ideas from the story that you had difficulty understanding. Write them on index cards. On the other side of the cards, explain how the read-on fix-up strategy helped you solve the problem.

Consonant Doubling in Context

Reread *Smart Food, Smart Choices, Healthy You!* to find examples of words that fit the consonant-doubling rule. Then use those words plus three additional consonant-doubling words to write a paragraph about healthy eating. Exchange paragraphs with a partner, and circle the words that fit the rule.

Turn and Talk

USE FIX-UP STRATEGIES: READ ON

Discuss with a partner what you have learned so far about how to use the read-on fix-up strategy.

- What does it mean to read on?

- How can the read-on strategy help you solve problems you encounter while reading?

Choose one problem you had while reading *Smart Food, Smart Choices, Healthy You!* Explain to a partner how the read-on fix-up strategy did or did not help you solve the problem.

Critical Thinking

With a group, brainstorm a list of smart foods. Return to *Smart Food, Smart Choices, Healthy You!* Write a definition of smart food. Then, discuss these questions together.

- How do smart foods differ from foods such as hamburgers, fries, pie, and soda?

- What is the author's argument in favor of smart foods?

The Organ Opera

Okay, I admit it. I love cartoons. I have a new favorite—*Organ Opera*. How can you not love a team of disease-fighting organs and a singing doctor? The team is always ready to **defend** good health. Each week Hank Heart, Louie and Larry Lung, Kelly and Kerry Kidney, and Dr. Gomez tackle another illness.

There is a great **basic** supporting cast. Hank Heart has an army of red and white blood cells from the **circulatory** system at his service. The Lung brothers call on members of the **respiratory** system. The Lung boys are forever moving oxygen into the red blood cells. They're very hard workers.

Dr. Gomez's **specialization** appears to be singing, not medicine. However, that doesn't stop him from going after any disease that crosses his path. In last week's show, a nasty cold laid the Lung boys low. The entire team rushed to their aid, but the stars of the show were the white blood cells—they had the infection under control in no time. Check out *Organ Opera*. I think you'll like it—and you'll learn something.

Structured Vocabulary Discussion

With a partner, say the vocabulary word that comes to mind when you hear the phrases below. Explain the reason for your choice.

majoring in biology at college

standing up to a bully

reading, writing, and arithmetic

track around football field

> Throughout the week, add to your vocabulary journal entries. Record new insights and other words that relate to this week's vocabulary.

Picture It

Copy this word wheel into your vocabulary journal. In the upper sections, name things that relate to the **respiratory** system. In the bottom sections, names things that are not related to the respiratory system.

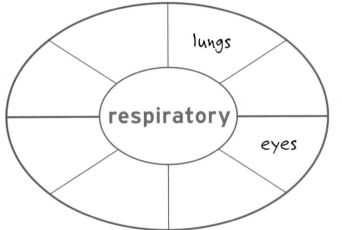

Copy this word organizer into your vocabulary journal. Fill in the ovals with words that mean the same as **specialization**, and in the boxes list examples of things that are a specialization.

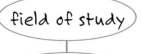

The CIRCULATORY Ride

by David Dreier

I slip and slide and try to hide,

I'm not ready for this circulatory ride.

I know the start will thrill my heart,

But I don't think the rush is all that smart.

A gentle float is more my speed.

I feel the pressure begin to mount,

One by one my steps I count.

The other blood cells laugh and shout,

Happily eager for the wild ride no doubt.

A gentle float is more my speed.

Miles of arteries, capillaries, and veins

Are the circulatory system's blood-filled lanes.

Outward bound arteries pound and gush,

But I much prefer the veins' lack of rush.

The gentle return home is more my speed.

I close my eyes and take the plunge,

At breakneck speed through the arteries I lunge.

Just when I think I can take no more,

The veins carry me back to my heart's door.

And although the trip started just minutes ago—

I'm in line to do it once more!

A Day in the Life of a
Red Blood Cell

Dear Diary,

What an exhausting day! I know I ran around the body a minimum of 1,440 times! I'm worn out. If I had known it was going to be this rough a day, I would have stayed in bed! It is days like today that make me appreciate what an important job I have. I guess I shouldn't complain—I knew I was in for a heavy workload when I took this assignment in the circulatory system.

My body was running in a marathon, so she needed a lot of extra oxygen. Each time she drew a breath, she had to quickly draw another. The lungs were so busy loading me and the other red blood cells with oxygen, that they barely had time to catch their breath. The last time they worked this hard in this kind of weather, they caught a cold. The heart and brain say that exercise is very important for our body. They say that it won't wear us out, but I'm not so sure. The brain and heart weren't the ones who had to run around the circulatory system so many times today!

R. B. Cell

Irregular Verbs

Activity One

About Irregular Verbs

An irregular verb is a verb that does not end in *-ed* when it shows past action or when it follows a helping verb. The word *do* is an example of an irregular verb. Its past tense form is *did*. The word *done* follows the helping verbs *have*, *has*, or *had*. As your teacher reads *A Day in the Life of a Red Blood Cell*, listen for irregular verbs.

Irregular Verbs in Context

With a partner, read *A Day in the Life of a Red Blood Cell* to find irregular verbs. Write down each irregular verb you find in a chart like the one below. Indicate each verb's present and past-tense forms.

PRESENT TENSE	PAST TENSE	VERB FORM WITH HELPING VERB
know	knew	has, have, or had known

Activity Two

Explore Words Together

With a partner, look at the list of verbs on the right. Take turns listing the various past tense forms of each word.

write	give
begin	choose
bite	ride

Activity Three

Explore Words in Writing

Write three additional sentences for R. B. Cell's diary entry using the present tense form of an irregular verb. Then, rewrite each sentence using the verb's past tense forms. Share your favorite sentence with a partner.

Something to Sneeze About!

by Tisha Hamilton

"Science is all about observation," Mrs. Figueroa told her fifth grade class. "So I want to start each class with an exercise that will teach observation skills. Turn to a clean page in your science notebook, and for the next five minutes write down anything your five senses tell you: sight, touch, smell, taste, and sound."

Tony opened his notebook and wrote the date at the top of the page. Mrs. Figueroa said, "Start now. I'll tell you when time is up." Then she opened the large terrarium that sat in front of the windows and began checking on her many plants.

Tony's pencil was coated in smooth yellow paint, so he wrote that down. He heard a small "Thunk!" Red-haired Alicia had dropped her pencil. Tony wrote it down. Over by the window someone coughed. Then there was a click as Mrs. Figueroa replaced the lid of the terrarium. Tony stuck the end of his pencil in his mouth, but it didn't taste like anything so he didn't write that down. Next to Tony, Rodney uncapped his marker, and Tony wrote about the marker smell in his notebook.

How does the illustration on this page help you understand the text?

Once Mrs. Figueroa called, "Time," it was fun to compare everyone's efforts. Some students wrote about birds chirping outside the classroom. Others wrote about changes in the window light as clouds passed across the sun. When Serena told about hearing her stomach gurgle, everyone laughed.

"Observation is important in all science, no matter what the area of specialization," Mrs. Figueroa explained. "It's important to pay attention to everything, because you never know what may turn out to be important later on."

How do the illustrations help you visualize Tony's sensory observations?

Tony thought it was an interesting exercise. He liked Mrs. Figueroa and he liked science class. When the bell rang he was sorry to have to leave science for his next subject. But by the next day Tony's opinion of science class was beginning to change. It started not long after he walked into the classroom and sat down. *Ah-choo! Aaaaah-choo!* He sneezed violently several times in a row.

"Tony, are you all right?" Mrs. Figueroa wanted to know. "Would you like to go to the nurse?"

Tony thought about it. He felt fine. He just couldn't seem to stop sneezing. Besides, he liked science. He decided to stay, but so did his sneezing fit.

Say Something Technique Take turns reading a section of text, covering it up, and then saying something about it to your partner. You may say any thought or idea that the text brings to your mind.

As he walked to his next class, Tony worried that he might be getting sick. He hated having a cold. Also, this week they were starting a new science unit and he didn't want to miss the beginning of it.

The sneezing seemed to stop once he left Mrs. Figueroa's room, though, and for the rest of the day he was fine.

The next day, though, the sneezing started up all over again as soon as Tony walked into science class. Mrs. Figueroa looked perplexed as she scratched at a red spot on her right hand. "I'm beginning to think there must be something in the air in my classroom," she said. "Sneezing, like coughing, is a reaction to an irritant in the respiratory system."

"You mean like the way I'm allergic to tree pollen," Rodney clarified. "That makes me sneeze in the spring, but it doesn't bother anyone else in my family."

"Exactly," said Mrs. Figueroa. "Let's see if we can be the scientists who discover what is causing Tony's sneezing fits."

How do your mental images of the story compare with the illustrations? Explain your answer.

What mental images do you have based on the illustrations for this page?

"It must be something only I am allergic to," Tony pointed out. "No one else is sneezing."

"And it must be something that's new or different in the classroom," Alicia added, "because Tony wasn't sneezing last week."

"What if we start by looking at our science notebooks?" Molly suggested. "Maybe if we compare our observations from one day to another we can figure out what changed."

"That's an excellent idea!" Mrs. Figueroa exclaimed.

The classroom was silent while everyone pored over their notebooks. Rodney got up to sharpen his pencil at the sharpener on the windowsill. The grinding of the sharpener was followed by the sound of coughing. Rodney coughed and covered his mouth in the way they'd been taught in school to keep from spreading any germs. By the time he got back to his seat, his coughing had stopped.

That reminded Tony of something. He remembered writing about someone coughing the other day. He flipped back in his science notebook. Sure enough, someone over by the window had coughed. Then today, Rodney coughed when he was in pretty much the same place. Could this be a clue?

The coughing was the same, but Tony was also looking for something that was different. Finally something clicked. Or rather, it didn't click. "I think I know what's different, Mrs. Figueroa," Tony said slowly. "Three days ago you replaced the lid on the terrarium after you checked the plants," he went on. "But today the lid is off the terrarium."

"That's right," Mrs. Figueroa admitted. "Yesterday morning when I came in I noticed a lot of condensation on the terrarium walls. I decided to leave the lid off for a few days so the moisture could evaporate."

"And just now when I was over by the terrarium, I started coughing," Rodney put in.

"And three days ago someone else coughed when Mrs. Figueroa had the lid off the terrarium," Tony finished.

"I was coughing," Mrs. Figueroa said. "I remember feeling a tickle in my throat when I was touching one of the plants."

"The same plant that gave you that rash?" Tony asked.

Mrs. Figueroa beamed. "Scientific observation saves the day," she said. "I wondered what was causing that rash! Over the weekend I added a new plant. Why don't we look up its properties? But first let's put the lid back on the terrarium."

How did the illustrations in this story help you understand details about the mystery?

Think and Respond

Listen and Write

- You and your partner took turns reading sections of *Something to Sneeze About!* and sharing your thoughts and ideas. Discuss one of your favorite thoughts and explain how the text brought it to your mind.

- On an index card, write a description of one of the illustrations from the story. On the other side of the card, write down how that illustration helped you understand the text.

Irregular Verbs in Context

Reread *Something to Sneeze About!* to find examples of irregular verbs. Write down the examples you find. Then use the verbs in a short newspaper article describing how Mrs. Figueroa's class solved the mystery of Tony's sneezing. Share your article with the class.

Turn and Talk Review

CREATE IMAGES: USE VISUALS

What have you learned so far about using visuals?

- How does using visuals to create mental images help you get more from what you read?

Choose one of the mental images you created while reading *Something to Sneeze About!* Explain to a partner how that image helped you unravel the mystery in the story.

Critical Thinking

In a group, discuss what you know about mystery stories. Return to *Something to Sneeze About!* Brainstorm with your group a list of clues that helped you unravel the mystery. Write down the clues on a piece of paper, and circle the clues that are visual. Then discuss these questions together.

- When did Tony start sneezing?

- What clues can you find in the first illustration that foreshadow the mystery's solution?

- How did Mrs. Figueroa's class go about solving the mystery?

Glossary

Using the Glossary

Like a dictionary, this glossary lists words in alphabetical order. Guide words at the top of each page show you the first and last word on the page. If a word has more than one syllable, the syllables are separated by a dark dot (•). Use the pronunciation key on the bottom of every other page.

Sample

The pronunciation guide shows how to say the word. The accent shows which syllable is stressed.

The part of speech shows how the word is often used.

Each word is broken into syllables.

in•fec•tions (in fek´ shəns) *pl. n.* Diseases caused by germs, bacteria, or other means. *Washing a cut can help prevent* **infections**.

The definition shows what the word means.

The example sentence includes the word in it.

Abbreviations: *adj.* adjective, *adv.* adverb, *conj.* conjunction, *interj.* interjection, *n.* noun, *prep.* preposition, *pron.* pronoun, *v.* verb

accomplished • cytoplasm

ac•com•plished (ə käm´ plisht) *v.* Completed or achieved. *I* **accomplished** *my goal of reading four books over the summer.*

ad•vance•ment (ad vans´ mənt) *n.* Progress or improvement. *The invention of the computer was a great* **advancement** *in technology.*

ad•ver•tise•ment (ad´ vər tīz´ mənt) *n.* A paid announcement about a product, need, or service. *The* **advertisement** *was trying to sell a new type of toothpaste.*

al•ler•gic (ə lur´ jik) *adj.* Having an allergy, or physical reaction, to something. *I am* **allergic** *to cats and dogs; they make me sneeze.*

ar•ro•gant (ar´ ə gənt) *adj.* Full of pride or a feeling of self–importance. *The new soccer player had an* **arrogant** *attitude that the other players did not have.*

ar•ti•fi•cial (är´ tə fi´ shəl) *adj.* Made by human work, not by nature. *The room was filled with* **artificial** *plants.*

com•mu•ni•ca•tions (kə myoo´ ni kā´ shəns) *pl. n.* A system for sending and receiving information, signals, or messages. *The telephone is an important means of* **communications.**

cy•to•plasm (si´ tō pla´ zəm) *n.* The material inside a cell that surrounds the nucleus. **Cytoplasm** *is a jelly-like material.*

de·fi·nite·ly (deˊ fə nit lē) *adv.* Clearly or certainly. *The dog was **definitely** friendly.*

des·ti·na·tion (desˊ tə nāˊ shən) *n.* The place toward which someone or something is going or is sent. *Our **destination** was the state park.*

DNA (dēˊ enˊ āˊ) *n.* The material in a cell that contains the characteristics of the cell; how characteristics are transferred from parent to child. *The color of your eyes is determined by your **DNA**.*

en·thu·si·as·ti·cal·ly (en thoōˊ zē asˊ tik lē) *adv.* Eagerly, with much interest. *I cheered **enthusiastically** for my team.*

ex·act (eg zaktˊ) *adj.* Specific; without mistake. *This is the **exact** amount to buy my lunch.*

ex·cel (ek selˊ) *v.* To be better at something than other people. *If I practice, I can **excel** at tennis.*

ex·plo·ra·tion (eksˊ plə rāˊ shən) *n.* The act of traveling to unknown or little known places in order to learn about them. *Space **exploration** is helping us learn more about the planets.*

fa·tigued (fə tēgdˊ) *v.* Having been made or having become tired. *We were **fatigued** after our long hike.*

fun·da·men·tal (funˊ də menˊ təl) *n.* Basic rule or skill. *Knowing how to move the stone is a **fundamental** in curling.*

hos·tile (häsˊ təl) *adj.* Unfriendly, showing dislike. *The crowd was **hostile** toward the opposing team.*

im·age (imˊ ij) *n.* A picture or likeness of a person, place, or object. *The **image** in the glass window mirrored the buildings and the street.*

im·pass·a·ble (im pasˊ ə bəl) *adj.* Cannot be passed, crossed, or traveled over. *The road was **impassable** after the storm.*

in·fec·tions (in fekˊ shəns) *pl. n.* Diseases caused by germs, bacteria, or other means. *Washing a cut can help prevent **infections**.*

in·ju·ry (inˊ jə rē) *n.* Physical harm to a person or property. *The boy's **injury** was not serious.*

in·tense (in tensˊ) *adj.* Very strong. *The pressure to succeed was **intense**.*

ir·ri·tant (irˊ i tənt) *adj.* Something that causes pain, a lack of comfort, or anger. *The noise of the machinery was a constant **irritant**.*

PRONUNCIATION KEY

a	add, map	oi	oil, boy	zh	vision, pleasure
ā	ace, rate	ou	pout, now	ə	the schwa, an
â(r)	care, air	ŏŏ	took, full		unstressed vowel
ä	palm, father	ōō	pool, food		representing the
e	end, pet	u	up, done		sound spelled
ē	equal, tree	ʉ	her, sir,		*a* in *above*
i	it, give		burn, word		*e* in *sicken*
ī	ice, write	yōō	fuse, few		*i* in *possible*
o	odd, hot	z	zest, wise		*o* in *melon*
ō	open, so				*u* in *circus*
ô	order, jaw				

me·cha·ni·cal (mə kaʹ ni kəl) *adj.* Produced or operated by machinery. *The **mechanical** dog could roll over and sit up.*

mem·brane (memʹ brānʹ) *n.* A thin sheet or layer serving as a covering. *A cell has an outer **membrane.***

men·tal (menʹ təl) *adj.* Of or in the mind. *Solving the problem took a great deal of **mental** effort.*

nu·cle·us (noōʹ klē əs) *n.* The part of a cell that contains the DNA and controls growth. *Most plant and animal cells have a **nucleus.***

parched (pärchd) *v.* Having been made hot, dry, or thirsty. *I was **parched** after mowing the grass.*

per·fec·tion (pər fekʹ shən) *n.* The condition of being perfect. *Adam's dive from the high board was **perfection.***

pos·si·bil·i·ty (päʹ sə bilʹ ə tē) *n.* The condition of being possible. *The weather station said there was a strong **possibility** of rain.*

quest (kwest) *n.* A search for something, a hunt. *My **quest** for the perfect gift took all day.*

ra·tions (raʹ shəns) *n.* Food or food supplies. *The explorers were almost out of **rations** by the time they crossed the mountain.*

re·sist·ance (ri zisʹ təns) *n.* The act of fighting or working against. *When he turned the corner, Ben could feel his bicycle slow down because of the wind **resistance.***

re·tire·ment (ri tīrʹ mənt) *n.* Leaving the work or business world because of age. *My grandmother and grandfather are enjoying their **retirement.***

scanned (skand) *v.* Looked through or read something quickly. *We **scanned** the newspaper to see if it mentioned our soccer game.*

sta·mi·na (staʹ mə nə) *n.* Ability to keep going; strength. *Kisha knew she had the **stamina** to finish the race.*

tech·no·lo·gy (tek näʹ lə jē) *n.* The development and use of technical knowledge and tools. *We have the **technology** to explore space.*

trans·form (trans fôrmʹ) *v.* To change the form or appearance of something. *I will **transform** the lump of clay into a bowl.*

trans·mit·ter (trans miʹ tər) *n.* A device or machine that sends a signal by radio waves or electric current. *The radio **transmitter** helped the scientists track the birds.*

vac·u·ole (vak´ yōo ōl´) *n.* A part of the cell that stores food, water, and waste. *The **vacuole** is a cell's storage area.*

va·ri·e·ty (və rī´ ə tē) *n.* A number of different kinds of something. *The garden had a **variety** of flowers.*

vi·nyl (vī´ nəl) *n.* A type of plastic. *At one time, most music was recorded on **vinyl** records.*

vir·tu·al (vur´ chōo əl) *adj.* Simulated by a computer to be something in effect, although not it actually. *A **virtual** globe is not actually a physical globe, but it serves the same purpose.*

vi·ta·mins (vī´ tə mins) *pl. n.* Chemicals found in food that are needed by the body for good health. *I get **vitamins** by eating fruits and vegetables.*

PRONUNCIATION KEY

a	add, map	oi	oil, boy	zh	vision, pleasure
ā	ace, rate	ou	pout, now	ə	the schwa, an
â(r)	care, air	ŏŏ	took, full		unstressed vowel
ä	palm, father	ōō	pool, food		representing the
e	end, pet	u	up, done		sound spelled
ē	equal, tree	ŧ	her, sir,		*a* in *above*
i	it, give		burn, word		*e* in *sicken*
ī	ice, write	yōō	fuse, few		*i* in *possible*
o	odd, hot	z	zest, wise		*o* in *melon*
ō	open, so				*u* in *circus*
ô	order, jaw				

Acknowledgements

For permission to reprint copyrighted material, grateful acknowledgment is made to the following sources:

America's Champion Swimmer: Gertrude Ederle by David Adler. Text © 2000 by Terry Widener, reproduced by permission of Harcourt, Inc.

Bewildered for Three Days by Andrew Glass. Copyright © 2000 by Andrew Glass. All rights reserved. Reprinted from *Bewildered for Three Days: As to Why Daniel Boone Never Wore His Coonskin Cap* by permission of Holiday House, Inc.

from *Edison's Fantastic Phonograph* by Diana Kimpton, illustrated by M. P. Robertson. Text © 2003 by Diana Kimpton. Illustrations © 2003 by M. P. Robertson. Published by Frances Lincoln Children's Books. Reproduced by permission of Frances Lincoln Ltd., 4 Torriano Mews, Torriano Avene, London NW5 2RZ.

from *The Heart: Our Circulatory System* by Seymour Simon. Text © 1996 by Seymour Simon. Reprinted by permission of Morrow Junior Books. All rights reserved.

June 29, 1999 by David Wiesner. Copyright © 1992 by David Wiesner. Reprinted by permission of Clarion Books, an imprint of Houghton Mifflin Company. All rights reserved.

from *Mirette on the High Wire* by Emily Arnold McCully. Copyright © 1992 by Emily Arnold McCully. Used by permission of G. P. Putnam's Sons, A division of Penguin Young Readers Group, A Member of Penguin Group (USA) Inc., 345 Hudson Street, New York, NY 10014. All rights reserved.

Queen of Inventions: How the Sewing Machine Changed the World by Laurie Carlson. Text © 2003 by Laurie Carlson. Published by permission of The Millbrook Press, Inc. All rights reserved.

from *The Way West: Journal of a Pioneer Woman* by Amelia Stewart Knight, illustrated by Michael McCurdy. Text © 1993 by Simon & Schuster, Inc. Illustrations © 1993 by Michael McCurdy. Reprinted by permission of Simon & Schuster Books for Young Readers, an Imprint of Simon & Schuster Children's Publishing Division. All rights reserved.

Unit Opener Acknowledgements

P.256a ©The Granger Collection New York; p.318a ©Erich Lessing/Art Resource, NY; p.380a ©The Jacob and Gwendolyn Lawrence Foundation/Art Resource, NY; p.442a ©The Georgia O'Keeffe Museum, Santa Fe, New Mexico, U.S.A./Art Resource, NY.

Illustration Acknowledgements

P.262c Tom McKee/Wilkinson Studios; p.266a Tammy Smith/Wilkinson Studios; p.267c S.G. Brooks/Wilkinson Studios; p.267d S.G. Brooks/Wilkinson Studios; p.270a Bradley Clark/Wilkinson Studios; p.272a Bradley Clark/Wilkinson Studios; p.274a Bradley Clark/Wilkinson Studios; p.278a Helle Urban/Wilkinson Studios; p.280a Burgandy Beam/Wilkinson Studios; p.282a S.G. Brooks/Wilkinson Studios; p.284a S.G. Brooks/Wilkinson Studios; p.285a Rebecca Peed/Wilkinson Studios; p.286a S.G. Brooks/Wilkinson Studios; p.286a S.G. Brooks/Wilkinson Studios; p.292a Chris Pappas/Wilkinson Studios; p.292b Chris Pappas/Wilkinson Studios; p.292d Chris Pappas/Wilkinson Studios; p.293c Chris Pappas/Wilkinson Studios; p.300a Bradley Clark/Wilkinson Studios; p.302a Bradley Clark/Wilkinson Studios; p.304a Bradley Clark/Wilkinson Studios; p.304c Bradley Clark/Wilkinson Studios; p.308a Brad Teare/Wilkinson Studios; p.312a Vicki Bradley/Wilkinson Studios; p.314a Vicki Bradley/Wilkinson Studios; p.316a Vicki Bradley/Wilkinson Studios; p.317b Vicki Bradley/Wilkinson Studios; p.324a Stephen Reed/Wilkinson Studios; p.328a Helle Urban/Wilkinson Studios; p.332a Paula Wendland-Zinngrabe/Wilkinson Studios; p.334a Paula Wendland-Zinngrabe/Wilkinson Studios; p.336a Paula Wendland-Zinngrabe/Wilkinson Studios; p.337a Paula Wendland-Zinngrabe/Wilkinson Studios; p.342d Geoffrey Paul Smith/Wilkinson Studios; p.343d Geoffrey Paul Smith/Wilkinson Studios; p.344a Jerry Tiritilli/Wilkinson Studios; p.344c Chris Pappas/Wilkinson Studios; p.344c Chris Pappas/Wilkinson Studios; p.344d Chris Pappas/Wilkinson Studios; p.344d Chris Pappas/Wilkinson Studios; p.346a Jerry Tiritilli/Wilkinson Studios; p.348a Jerry Tiritilli/Wilkinson Studios; p.358a Stan Gorman/Wilkinson Studios; p.365c Thomas Gagliano/Wilkinson Studios; p.370a Judith Hunt-King/Wilkinson Studios; p.374a Jim Kilmartin/Wilkinson Studios; p.374d Jim Kilmartin/Wilkinson Studios; p.375b Jim Kilmartin/Wilkinson Studios;

p.375d Michael DiGiorgio/Wilkinson Studios; p.376a Jim Kilmartin/Wilkinson Studios; p.376d Jim Kilmartin/Wilkinson Studios; p.378a Michael DiGiorgio/Wilkinson Studios; p.378b Jim Kilmartin/Wilkinson Studios; p.378d Jim Kilmartin/Wilkinson Studios; p.386b Jared Osterhold/Wilkinson Studios; p.386b Jared Osterhold/Wilkinson Studios; p.386c Jared Osterhold/Wilkinson Studios; p.386c Jared Osterhold/Wilkinson Studios; p.386d Jared Osterhold/Wilkinson Studios; p.387d Jared Osterhold/Wilkinson Studios;

p.391b Thomas Gagliano/Wilkinson Studios; p.392a George Hamblin/Wilkinson Studios; p.394a Brian Miller/Wilkinson Studios; p.395a Brian Miller/Wilkinson Studios; p.396a Brian Miller/Wilkinson Studios; p.397a Brian Miller/Wilkinson Studios; p.398a Brian Miller/Wilkinson Studios; p.399a Brian Miller/Wilkinson Studios; p.402a Jeff Grunewald/Wilkinson Studios; p.402b Jeff Grunewald/Wilkinson Studios; p.404a Jared Osterhold/Wilkinson Studios; p.404a Jared Osterhold/Wilkinson Studios; p.406a Julie Bauknecht/Wilkinson Studios; p.408a Julie Bauknecht/Wilkinson Studios; p.410a Julie Bauknecht/Wilkinson Studios; p.420a Cheryl Cook/Wilkinson Studios; p.422a Robert Van Nood/Wilkinson Studios; p.423a Robert Van Nood/Wilkinson Studios; p.428d Georhe Hamblin/Wilkinson Studios; p.430a Dan Bridy/Wilkinson Studios; p.431c Dan Bridy/Wilkinson Studios; p.432a Cynthia Sears/Wilkinson Studios; p.434a Dan Bridy/Wilkinson Studios; p.436a Julie Olson/Wilkinson Studios; p.438a Julie Olson/Wilkinson Studios; p.440a Julie Olson/Wilkinson Studios; p.441a Julie Olson/Wilkinson Studios; p.448b Tom Katsulis/Wilkinson Studios; p.456a Angel Mosquito/Wilkinson Studios; p.458a Angel Mosquito/Wilkinson Studios; p.460a Angel Mosquito/Wilkinson Studios; p.461a Angel Mosquito/Wilkinson Studios; p.464a Jenny Sylvaine/Wilkinson Studios; p.470d Tony Boisvert/Wilkinson Studios; p.471b Tony Boisvert/Wilkinson Studios; p.472c Annamarie Boley/Wilkinson Studios; p.482a Ron Mahoney/Wilkinson Studios; p.486a Helle Urban/Wilkinson Studios; p.486a Helle Urban/Wilkinson Studios; p.492b Bob Brugger/Wilkinson Studios; p.494a Nadine Sokol/Wilkinson Studios; p.496b Jared Osterhold/Wilkinson Studios; p.496c Jared Osterhold/Wilkinson Studios; p.498a Cynthia Watts Clark/Wilkinson Studios; p.500a Cynthia Watts Clark/Wilkinson Studios; p.502a Cynthia Watts Clark/Wilkinson Studios; p.503a Cynthia Watts Clark/Wilkinson Studios.

Photography Acknowledgements

P.262b Element Photo Shoot; p.262a ©Pat & Chuck Blackley; p.263c ©Barry Rosenthal/Getty Images; p.265d Element Photo Shoot; p.265d Element Photo Shoot; p.266a ©Bettmann/Corbis, TSP 49; p.266c ©Getty Images, TSP 49; p.266d ©Robert Holmes/Corbis, TSP 49; p.267a ©Ansel Adams Publishing Rights Trust/Corbis, TSP 50; p.268a ©James Frank/Alamy; p.268d ©North Wind/North Wind Picture Archives; p.375d ©Scott T. Smith/Corbis; p.276b ©Connie Ricca/Corbis; p.277c ©Associated Press, U.S. MINT; p.280b Courtesy of the United States Postal Service; p.280d ©Bettmann/Corbis; p.281d ©Ann Ronan Picture Library/HIP/The Image Works; p.288d ©North Wind/North Wind Picture Archives; p.295d Element Photo Shoot; p.296a ©Tom Bean/Corbis, TSP 55; p.296b ©Bettmann/Corbis, TSP 55; p.297d ©Getty Images, TSP 56; p.298a ©Element Photo Shoot; p.298a ©David Muench/Corbis; p.298d ©Western History/Genealogy Dept., Denver Public Library; p.299d ©Raymond Bial/www.raybial.com; p.305b ©Michael T. Sedam/Corbis; p.306b ©Denver Public Library; p.307c ©Denver Public Library; p.310b ©Craig Aurness/Corbis; p.310d Photograph is courtesy of the NPS National Trails System, Salt Lake City Office; p.311b ©Smithsonian National Postal Museum; p.320d ©Duomo/Corbis; p.325c ©Alain Nogues/Corbis Sygma; p.327c Element Photo Shoot; p.329a Element Photo Shoot; p.329b Element Photo Shoot; p.329d ©Peter Arnold, Inc./Alamy, TSP 62; p.330a Element Photo Shoot 2nd use; p.330b ©Hulton Archive/Getty Images; p.330c ©NASA/Roger Ressmeyer/Corbis; p.330d ©James A. Sugar/National Geographic Image Collection; p.338a Element Photo Shoot; p.338d ©Roger Ressmeyer/Corbis; p.339c ©Swerve/Alamy; p.340b ©Worldspec/NASA/Alamy; p.342a Element Photo Shoot; p.350b ©Michael Newman/Photo Edit; p.354b Element Photo Shoot; p.354a ©Chris Collins/Corbis 2nd use; p.354c ©Tony Freeman/Photo Edit; p.354d ©Manfred Gottschalk/lonelyplanetImages.com; p.357c Element Photo Shoot; p.360a Element Photo Shoot; p.360d ©Alistair Berg/Getty Images; p.362b ©Time & Life Pictures/Getty Images; p.362b ©Associated Press, United States Postal Service; p.362d ©Bettmann/Corbis; p.363b ©Associated Press, AP; p.363c ©Bettmann/Corbis; p.364a ©Associated Press, AP; p.364c ©Popperfoto/Alamy; p.364d ©Associated Press, AP; p.365b ©Associated Press, Yomiuri Shimbun; p.365d ©Craig Lovell/Corbis; p.366a ©Neal Preston/Corbis; p.366c ©Reuters/Corbis; p.366d ©Getty Images; p.368a Element Photo Shoot; p.368b ©Associated Press, AP; p.372a Element Photo Shoot; p.372b ©Reuters/Corbis; p.372c ©Associated Press, AP; p.372d ©Associated Press, The News Press; p.373d ©Associated Press, AP; p.382b ©Louie Psihoyos/Corbis; p.386b ©NMPFT/SSPL/The Image Works; p.386c ©Bettmann/Corbis;

p.386d ©Topham/The Image Works; p.387c ©John Springer Collection/Corbis; p.389d Element Photo Shoot; p.390d Element Photo Shoot; p.400a Element Photo Shoot; p.400a ©Bettmann/Corbis; p.400c ©Bettmann/Corbis; p.400c ©Getty Images; p.400a ©Corbis; p.401c ©SSPL/The Image Works; p.402c Courtesy of NASA; p.402c Courtesy of NASA;

p.402c ©USGS/MS Research Terra Server USA - Urban Area Ortho Imagery - Washington D.C. NASA; p.403b Courtesy of NASA; p.403b Courtesy of NASA; p.403d Courtesy of NASA; p.412b ©Anna Peisl/Getty Images; p.416b Photo Courtesy of Charles De Mestral; p.416b ©Scott Camazine/Photo Researchers, Inc.; p.416d ©Fogstock LLC/SuperStock; p.416d ©Dr. Jeremy Burgess/Photo Researchers, Inc.; p.416b ©David Boag/Alamy; p.417c ©Andrew McRobb/Dorling Kindersley; p.419d Element Photo Shoot; p.424b Element Photo Shoot; p.424c Element Photo Shoot; p.424d ©Courtesy of Microsoft Corp; p.425a Element Photo Shoot; p.425c ©Associated Press, AP; p.426c Element Photo Shoot; p.426b Element Photo Shoot 2nd use; p.426d Lakeside Photo courtesy of the Lakeside School; p.427a Element Photo Shoot; p.427c © Photo Courtesy of Microsoft Corp.; p.428b Element Photo Shoot 3rd use; p.428b Element Photo Shoot; p.428a ©Doug Wilson/Corbis; p.430d ©Paul Barton/Corbis; p.448d Element Photo Shoot; p.451d Element Photo Shoot; p.452a Element Photo Shoot; p.454a Element Photo Shoot; p.454b ©Bettmann/Corbis; p.454c ©The Granger Collection, New York; p.454d ©Omikron/Photo Researchers, Inc.; p.462a Element Photo Shoot; p.462d Element Photo Shoot; p.462b ©Adrienne Hart-Davis/Science Photo Library;

p.463c ©Michael Grant/Alamy; p.466a ©Ed Reschke/Peter Arnold, Inc; p.466b ©National Cancer Institute/Science Photo Library; p.466b ©Bo Veisland, MI&I /Science Photo Library; p.466c ©Russell Kightley/Science Photo Library; p.467b ©Russell Kightley/Science Photo Library; p.468a Element Photo Shoot; p.468b ©Dustin Hardin/Getty Images; p.468c ©Doug Steley/Alamy; p.469b ©Core Agency/Getty Images; p.469c ©Pascal Goetgheluck/Science Photo Library; p.470a Element Photo Shoot 2nd use; p.471a ©Dustin Hardin/Getty Images 2nd use; p.472a Element Photo Shoot 3rd use; p.472b ©Dustin Hardin/Getty Images 3rd use; p.476a ©2005 Doctor Stock; p.477b ©2005 Doctor Stock; p.478a Element Photo Shoot; p.478b ©Bo Veisland/Science Photo Library; p.478b ©David Gifford/Science Photo Library;

p.478c ©Reuters/Corbis; p.479c ©SIU/Science Photo Library; p.481c Element Photo Shoot; p.484a Element Photo Shoot; p.486d ©David Young-Wolff/Photo Edit; p.487d Courty of the USDA; p.488d ©Schnare & Stief/Stockfood; p.490c ©Patrik Giardino/Corbis; p.492a Element Photo Shoot; p.496a Element Photo Shoot.

Additional Photography by A&O Maksymenko/Shutterstock; Blend Images/Alamy; Brett Stoltz/Shutterstock; Comstock Royalty Free/Telescope; Corbis/Harcourt Index; Corbis Royalty Free/Telescope; Digital Studios/Telescope; Digital Zoo/Getty Images Royalty Free;

Dynamic Graphics Group/Creatas/Alamy; Edyta Pawlowska/Shutterstock; Getty Images/PhotoDisc/Harcourt Index; Getty Images Royalty Free /Telescope; Getty Images Royalty Free/Harcourt Index; Getty Images/PhotoDisc/Harcourt Index; Giovanna Tondelli/Shutterstock; Ingram Publishing Limited Royalty Free/Telescope; Jaimie Duplass/Shutterstock; Jeremy Hoare/Life File/Getty Images; Jose Luis Pelaez Inc/Getty Images Royalty Free; LWA/Dann Tardif/Getty Images; Mzagajewska/Dreamstime.com; Najin/Dreamstime.com; Paul Maguire/Shutterstock; Photick/Index Stock; Photos.com; Purestock /SuperStock; Royalty-Free/Corbis; Sruce2638/Dreamstime.com; Taolmor/Shutterstock; Yan Vugenfirer/Shutterstock.

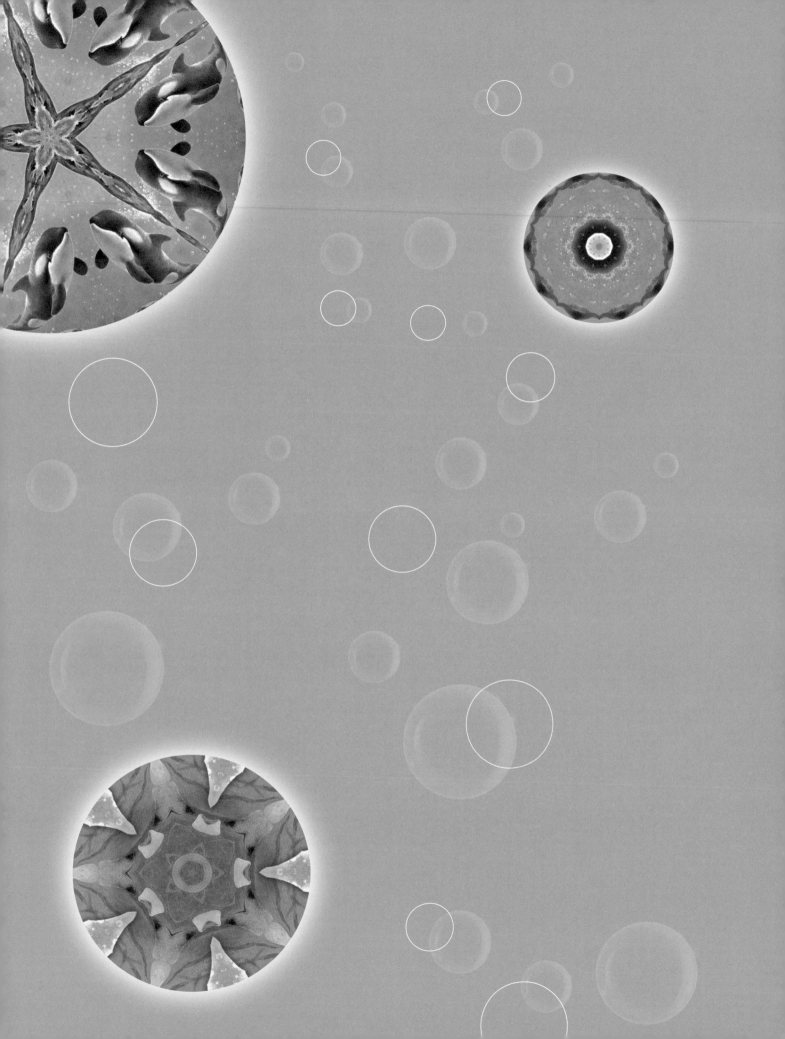